With thanks to David Rossi and Dan Lamb

Reliability of Rope

Samantha Priestley

Published by Armley Press 2015

Cover Design: Mick Lake

Layout: Ian Dobson

Contact: <info@armleypress.com>

ISBN 0-9554699-8-8

As I'm sure you already know Peter died last Tuesday. We are all quite well, really, and coping fine. The funeral will be on Wednesday (December 16th). You are very welcome to come.

Kate slid the note back into the hand-delivered envelope it had come in. An envelope with no address, just someone else's name. She put it down on the fireplace, still holding in her other hand a large square Christmas card that wasn't for her either.

Could it be the same Peter? Or was it a different Peter? How many Peters might have died on the same Tuesday? She turned the Christmas card over in her hand and looked at it again. Christmas cards were meant to be happy greetings, full of the children and grandchildren, this year's nativity, school, and summer holiday. Not deaths. Not like this one. But Peter was dead. That was it. 'Peter' had been dead for three days now. Since Tuesday. And now it was Friday, so he'd been cold and dead and still and quiet for more than two whole empty days. Was it the same Peter? She wondered about the woman who had lived here before, the woman the Christmas card was addressed to. Why would she have known the same Peter?

The front of the card showed a painting of an ice rink, kids in old brown clothes, hats and gloves, stolen mid-skate, one leg lazily held out behind each of them like a sleepily spoken word, and one adult skating with their hands held behind their back as if they were tied. Kate put her finger to the place on the picture where the woman's hands held each other at the base of her spine, free to let go and do whatever, whenever. It sloped into her brain as a happy scene, carefree, trusting, and it made Kate smile for a second. Before she remembered. Before she pulled the smile back into her mouth and remembered. She should be sombre. Peter was dead.

She opened the card again and read the cheerful Merry Christmas. No name above it for the person this card was meant for, just signed 'From Susie and Anthony'. It startled her again, a complete contrast to the note that lay encased in this happy message. How could they send this news in a Christmas card? Susie and Anthony. She wondered what relation they were to each other.

She pegged the card onto the cord that was stretched on the wall along with all the other ones she'd received so far this year, all the ones which were actually addressed to her and Matthew. Above the silver candle sticks on the coffee table, and the simple evenly spaced coasters, and the clear, clean, cream carpet. She stood back and looked at it. Nothing in the card itself to suggest it was a notification of a death. Confirmation of the end to Peter's life. No reason for anyone to think it told of a funeral, and that, despite it all, they were coping, they were well, Peter's family. She hoped it was true that Peter's family really were coping…

She looked at the way it perched, held on the cord by a little silver peg, skaters circling ice on the cover. The hands clasped behind the back. Then she turned away and picked up the phone to ring Matthew at work.

The phone rang three times and he answered, his deep southern voice sounding low and heavy in the line. "Hello?"

"Peter is dead," she said.

"Oh, I'm sorry to hear that."

"It's OK," she went on. "They are OK, apparently, even though he's dead. They say they are doing well, are fine."

"Well, that's something, I suppose."

*

Peter's grandfather had talked about the rope, and this place they lived in, as if the two things were inseparable. It was with them from birth. It hung in the air they breathed and decorated the landscape. It lay in bundles to be sold. It waited on hooks like a wreath, to be used.

"It's in our blood," he'd said, his stocky figure, his serious face, his rough and worn hands, all telling how this business had rubbed itself into him and was part of him. "Yours too," he'd said, motioning to Peter.

Long before Peter was born, the men stood and made the rope, their low voices talking of the sea and the need for money and their women. Or quiet for what seemed like hours while their fingers worked and their eyes watched, keeping patience even in their bodies. Only the sound of the twining, the pull and scratch of the hemp. They worked their hands till burns scored their skin and grazes itched. They stood with the flax wrapped around their waists like the thin arms of children, clinging to them, squeezing just a little, so that when their bodies were released they felt the relief of being able to breathe freely again, but also the loss of the comforting hug.

At other times, men made the nets that fishermen would cast out into the sea. The rope transformed into a thing of safety, of reassurance. The rope became as important to them as cattle.

*

She hunted down the black things in her wardrobe like a cat. As always, she never had anything suitable for the occasion. She picked through the colours with her eyes and she located all the darkest items. She watched them from a distance before she approached them, before she could even think about moving near and touching them. Dresses, vest tops, trousers, skirts, cardigans and sweaters. Only the black ones. Only the ones without any curl of colours in them at all. Like they were shadows, ghosts amongst the living. Like they were bad memories that no one wanted to see. Finally, she lifted them and looked at them closely.

Matthew was standing in the kitchen, leaning against the sink, eating cheese on toast, when Kate came back from shopping. She'd bought something black. Kate's wardrobe seemed to consist only of summer clothes, three-quarter-length jeans, gypsy skirts, T-shirts, with the odd cardigan and denim jacket thrown in for the change in the weather. Matthew said it showed optimism, that she only bought for warm weather. But Kate thought it was just hopefulness, and besides, where they lived, down on the bottom edge of England, the cold rarely bit them that hard, just the wind from the sea that circled the buildings sometimes.

Matthew was slowly turning the pages of the free local paper with one hand while the other held the cheese on toast hovering in the air near his face. He looked up at Kate and he quickly brushed the crumbs from the toast into the sink.

"Where've you been today?"

"Exmouth. Had to get something... for the funeral, you know."

The cheese on toast quivered in Matthew's hand as he stared at Kate, not wanting to push, not wanting not to.

"Funeral?" he asked.

"Yeah, Peter, I told you."

"Who's Peter anyway?" he said.

"What?"

"Peter. On the phone you said Peter's dead, and I didn't say anything, but... who the hell is Peter?"

Kate walked around the little table where they ate their meals and lay her shoulder bag down, the bulky items inside it – phone, purse, make-up – all relaxing and separating inside the fabric of the bag like the bones of a drugged dog.

"It's no one, it doesn't matter," she said.

"And you knew this person? You sounded a bit… shook up about it."

Kate shrugged. "Yeah well, he died didn't he? It's sad. Has it taken you all day to realise you didn't know who I was talking about?"

"I might have known him," Matthew answered. "I thought it must be someone we both knew and I'd remember, but then… I didn't remember anyone called Peter."

He watched her as she moved to the kitchen area, bent to the fridge and began bringing out items that would make a meal. Chicken. Butter. Carrots. She placed each one on the side by the sink.

"Is it someone from work?" he asked.

She looked up at him. "Huh?"

"The guy who died, is it someone from work? Cos I know you don't like to talk a lot about work, and that's fine, cos I don't either, who wants to talk about work? Bad enough that we have to go, without us talking about it all the time, but, you know, if you want to talk about it, if it's upset you or anything...

if that's why... if it has something to do with you... not being well just lately, you know, being off work, well you can talk to me."

She smiled. "It doesn't matter," she said. Then turned back to the fridge and peered in as if she'd find something in here she'd been looking for for ages. "Just forget it," she went on. "I should never have said anything."

The doctor's surgery was quiet. Only two other people sat waiting, hunched over in their seats, coats on and bags on the floor in front of them, as if they were ready to flee at any moment. Kate approached the reception and spoke her name quietly. She'd never done this before. Never seen a doctor with a problem like this before. But there was no way she could go back to work right now.

"Take a seat," the receptionist said.

Kate smiled and turned to the row of chairs. She sat down in the middle of the seats, away from the other two patients. She knotted her fingers in her lap and in her head she rehearsed what she would say. *I've not been sleeping... someone died and... I can't concentrate on anything, you see, I can't focus, it's not sleeping, I'm just so tired.*

The machine on the wall beeped and Kate looked up to see her name flashing in red letters. She picked up her bag and walked to the doctor's rooms. She felt the pull of indecision as she stood there. She could leave now. Turn around and walk away. This was stupid. She wasn't the sort. She didn't have problems like this. But it was just that, she couldn't go back to work. She couldn't.

When she entered the room the doctor looked up and smiled. Kate sat down.

"What can I do for you today?" the doctor asked.

"I'm not sleeping," Kate said.

The doctor sat back in his chair and looked at her.

"Any particular reason?"

"Well, someone died," Kate said. "And, the thing is, I can't stop thinking about it, and I can't sleep because..." She stopped and looked down into her lap.

The doctor waited for just a second, then said, "When you say *someone* died, someone close to you?"

Kate looked up and took a breath. She looked as if she was about to speak, but nothing came out. Tears welled in the corners of her eyes and she shook her head.

"It's perfectly normal," the doctor went on, "when you suffer a loss. I think you would benefit from some counselling."

"No!" Kate said. "I don't want to go to counselling. I just need some time."

"Are you sure? I really think it would help you to cope."

"No really, it's not that, it's just, I need some time and I can't face going back to work, so I just need... we weren't close, it's not like that, it's not like it was family or anything."

"I see," the doctor said. "Well, I can sign you off work with stress if that would help, but think about the counselling, you do seem very upset about this."

The doctor was signing the note for her, his pen flying over the sheet, his eyes on the paper.

"Yes," Kate said. "I am, but I think it's just... shock, you know." She was getting up to leave. She took the paper from the doctor and picked up her bag. "Thank you," she said. "It's hard because it was so sudden, and I feel responsible, but..." she'd said more than she'd meant to. She'd thought it would be quick and simple. She never thought she'd cry. The doctor was looking at her. "Thank you," she said again. "I'll be fine."

*

When Peter walked with his dog through the undercliff or in the quiet narrow streets in early morning, he remembered his grandfather. And he thought about how when he was a boy his grandfather's dog never had a lead. Just ran. Just walked beside him and never strayed. He remembered the animal lying out in the sun by the door and how it would leap when his grandfather came out, as if it had been waiting for him and doing nothing else. And he remembered the only time that dog had a leash. A tumour so large it swelled to the size of a football between the dog's front legs. It had grown, concealed for who knows how long. But now the dog became slow with it, wouldn't eat, couldn't run. Peter must have been about eight years old, but he remembered it so clearly, like it had only happened yesterday. He'd been at his grandparents' house, as he often was, but on this day the atmosphere was dimmed and subdued. His grandmother was in the kitchen and she eyed Peter carefully while he sat at the table. The dog was lying on the floor, quiet and hardly moving at all. Peter's grandfather came into the kitchen. He exchanged a quick glance with his wife, but neither of them spoke. Peter remembers the awful feeling of dread, of knowing something was about to happen, but not knowing what it was. His grandfather's face was still and he didn't speak, just took a length of rope and tied it in a slipknot around the dog's neck, then walked from the house. That was the only time Peter had ever seen the dog with a lead. His grandfather had returned later without the dog and would never speak about it at all.

*

Kate had bought a black dress. It was a satin slip that came above her knees, covered by a second layer of lace that decorated all the parts of her skin the slip didn't reach to. She put it on and looked at herself in the mirror. She smoothed down her dirty blonde hair with her hand and turned her head to the side. Matthew was in the living room where a large pot plant leaned over by the TV and towels lay in the creases of the window frames, taking excess liquid and storing it in their folds. Kate hated the towels that lay like cats, dingy from the rainwater and condensation. When she lifted them away to wring them out and wash them, she picked at them with her fingers and held them away from herself as if their stale-water smell would infect her. Kate wanted double glazing. She wanted new windows with plastic frames that she could wipe down weekly and that didn't leak and shudder in the wind. But she and Matthew couldn't afford to move to a house with double glazing. Like the clothes she'd just bought and most other things, there was no way they could make the money stretch to it.

She turned a little further and looked at herself from the side and then the back. Was it the kind of thing you wore when someone had died? Kate didn't know. She'd never been to a funeral before. Never had death touch her and bring her face to face with a coffin and the weeping of friends and family members before. She angled her head from side to side as she stared at herself in the mirror. Her thick hair made curves and the shape of the sea around her face and shoulders. You could wear this dress to a party, she thought. To a club. Maybe that was a good thing because she and Matthew didn't exactly have loads of money and so at least she could say she'd bought wisely. She'd chosen a dress that was not only suitable for funerals, but would also hold good for other social occasions. Of course she knew what Matthew would say. He'd say, what social occasions? And of course he'd be right.

She swept her hands down over the lace on her thighs. Then she took out the black pumps she'd also bought and fitted them over her feet. That was another good buy. Kate didn't even consider heels, although she'd looked at some in the shop and thought briefly how elegant they were, how good they look on a woman who can carry them off. Tall, slim, poised. Not like Kate. Kate could hardly walk in heels for ten minutes at a time, let alone spend the morning at a funeral in them. So the pumps were by far the better option. Besides, heels really would be a waste of money. Where did Kate ever go that required she wear heels?

She stared at herself some more. She looked the part, she thought. She easily looked like someone about to stand at a graveside and weep or sit in a church and listen with sadness while someone's life was recalled and placed in the past. She wondered about jewellery, but decided it might be a bit inappropriate. No, she looked good like this. She was ready for it.

*

The man stood in his bedroom and held open his wardrobe door. He pushed his hair behind his ear, away from his pool-blue eyes, and trailed his hand down over the straggly mass of hair that he had been allowing to grow on his chin since the day his dad had died last week.

Everyone seemed to think he was still a boy, seemed to

treat him like one. But he was 25 now. And the beard was there to remind the world that, actually yes, I'm not just a teenager any more. So even if his mum did want to take issue with it, the beard was coming to the funeral too.

His mother wanted him to wear a suit. Of course she did. She wanted him to look the part. Respectful. Respectable. But he wasn't really bothered about being either of those things. Besides, he didn't own a suit of his own.

The only thing he could do was to go as himself. That was the only way he could be honest with his dad when he faced him for this last time. Just dressing up in a suit wouldn't have the power to take away all the guilt he felt piled up inside him about what had happened.

He let his hand wander over the items in his wardrobe. T-shirts. A couple of long-sleeved shirts. Two pairs of jeans. One pair of shorts. He couldn't see what the big deal was. His father was dead. He was gone now. What did it matter what Anthony was wearing on the day they buried him?

Still, his mother said, you have to wear a suit. Apparently, it's the done thing, she insisted, all the other men would be wearing a suit, Anthony's brothers would be wearing suits. Seemed to Anthony like another good reason not to wear one.

What's more, the outfit his mother had chosen for him seemed neither respectable nor respectful anyway. When she'd brought the black suit into his room yesterday, he'd just stared at her like it had to be a joke or something.

"He hardly wore it," she said. "And he certainly hasn't worn it for years."

"But it's *his* suit," Antony answered. "You can't be serious."

"Well, maybe if you owned one yourself we wouldn't have this problem!" she shouted. "I've got enough on without worrying about what you're going to wear. Go and hire one. Or just wear this!" she said, holding his father's suit out to him again. "I don't care. And shave off that ridiculous beard. Just... make an effort. Please."

Make an effort. She actually said, make an effort. Make

an effort with what? Dressing up in the correct way to please everyone else? For appearances? How would that help? Is that what really mattered? Appearances? It wouldn't help Anthony, or his mother, not really. She might think it mattered, but it didn't. None of that stuff mattered anymore. His father was dead. And no amount of shaving or dressing up in his dad's clothing could change that. It was too late. The time Anthony could have done anything about it had passed. If only he hadn't let things get as bad as they had been with his dad during the past few months.

But now it was too late. So the beard was to show his dad that he was making a new start, and the clothes were to show him he was still the same Anthony.

So what if his mother couldn't understand that? It was his dad's day tomorrow. He pulled his pale-blue jeans from the wardrobe, hung them on the open door ready for the morning, and began the task of finding a plain T-shirt that didn't need a wash.

*

Early on Wednesday morning Kate lay awake in bed before the alarm clock went off. She couldn't remember the name of the woman who had lived here before. M. Hooper. But what did the M stand for? Finally she crept out of bed and went searching in the black file she kept in the bottom of the wardrobe. She flicked her fingers through bills and bank statements, passports and birth certificates, all kept in order by date and importance, until she came to the scrap of paper the previous tenant of this flat had left behind when she moved out. That was about six months ago. Matthew had been living in this flat for a few weeks by himself before Kate moved in, so Kate hadn't met the woman the one time she came to pick up post that was still being delivered to this address. Some post had continued to arrive for M. Hooper since then. Subscription to a film review magazine she hadn't got around to cancelling. Catalogue for leather sofas. Credit card companies begging for her custom. An invitation to join the National Trust. But M. Hooper had never been back.

Kate read through the details on the paper again now.

Melanie. That was the woman's name. The woman who used to cook in this kitchen and walk in this hallway, climb the stairs and sleep in this bedroom before Matthew and Kate did. Melanie. Kate held the paper close to her body and scrunched it slightly in her fist. Behind her Matthew was waking, running his hand through the explosion of dark hair that spiked about on his head.

"What are you doing?" he asked.

Kate got to her feet. "Nothing," she said. "Don't forget I'm going to that thing today, so I don't know what time I'll be back."

"What thing?"

"Funeral. I told you."

She looked at the scrap of paper in her hand again. Melanie. The woman who used to live here. The woman the Christmas card was addressed to; a woman Kate had never met. And even though Kate had the invitation meant for Melanie, there was still a chance Melanie would be there today. But a little thing like that wasn't going to put her off: Kate would look out for her and, if she was there, make out that they knew each other, keep one step ahead of her. Nothing was going to keep Kate away; now she knew about the funeral she knew she had to be there. After all, in a village this size it had to be the same Peter. How many Peters could have died on the same Tuesday?

"Come back to bed."

She turned around and saw Matthew leaning on one side in the bed, his arm outstretched towards her.

"I can't," she said. "I've got to get ready."

"Come on, five more minutes won't hurt."

She looked at him from beneath her eyelashes. "Except it won't be just five minutes, will it? It's OK for you, all you do is throw your overalls on and go."

Kate got to her feet. "Anyway, I'm going to a funeral today." She began walking out of the bedroom. "It just wouldn't be *right*."

As she heard Matthew protesting she did stop for the briefest moment and considered going back, sliding into the bed and undressing, like she used to. But nothing was like it used to be anymore.

*

Susie put in her earrings, smoothed her long black skirt down, and then went into the kitchen and turned a half-full mug of coffee into the sink. She'd been short with Anthony last night. She knew she had, but didn't she have enough to think about...?

And he was old enough now to organise himself properly without her having to do everything for him. Today of all days, couldn't he just fall in line and behave like an adult? If he didn't come down those stairs wearing that suit...

She took a deep breath. It would be time to go soon. The car would be here and she'd have to sit there with the coffin up ahead of her. That was going to be the hardest thing, looking at it, watching it lying there and knowing Peter was inside. Although of course he was gone and that was just his body, she knew that. She knew he was gone, but all the same... it was going to be so hard.

And it was not as if the funeral would give her any answer to the nagging question in her head.

Why?

Her brain was still struggling to make any sense of it. Even though she tried to stop herself, she couldn't. She was asking herself all the time. The question just went round in her head on a loop.

Why did he have to die?

He hadn't even reached retirement age. Susie had always had an image in her head of the two of them retiring together, spending their days walking by the coast and taking quiet holidays abroad, but now everything had changed and there was no future she could imagine at all.

All she could see now was the body just where she had found it.

Why?

Why did this have to happen to her?

Why?

Why had he done this to her?

*

She'd watched Matthew walk away from the flat with his bag in his hand. The white overalls that were folded inside the bag were swiped with different colours. Paint that had been misdirected at his own body on the brush, instead of the wall or the door. Paint in swoops of red and terracotta, nut brown and aquamarine. Kate would sometimes unfold his overalls from the bag at the end of the day to wash them and would turn the different lengths of the fabric over in her palms, gazing at all these colours and wondering what the insides of these people's houses looked like. She imagined they were large houses with land around them and expensive cars parked on the driveway. She imagined Matthew inside these houses, painting the walls and ceilings, splattering his overalls every now and then and taking a piece of the atmosphere away with him at the end of the day. She didn't imagine the other, more mundane places he painted.

He walked down the narrow little road now, where he would wait at the end for the van to pick him up and take him to work. Kate watched Matthew from the window. His bag slung over his shoulder. Ruffle of black hair blowing in a lift of breeze.

*

Inside the department store the lights lit the space like a theatre. Matthew looked up at the tiled ceiling, the corners where it met the walls, the pillars, the shadows, the paint flaked and cobwebbed and dulled by time and dirty air. The building was empty, but full of the ghosts of conversations of shoppers and staff. Scent still lingering by the counters. A faint memory of yesterday's lasagne played by the escalator near the restaurant. The escalators had shut down, strangely muted and still. The place was like an empty church, or a derelict house, or a morgue.

Matthew and his work-mate stood for a moment and

looked at the walls up above the lifts. It was easy to see, even from down here, where the severe rain had forced its way in and caused its damage. The ceiling had been repaired and they had to get all the painting done today so the store could be reopened. Christmas was getting closer every day and the job needed to be done urgently.

Matthew stared up. It was high, but he could see where he had to go. They would get up there and do the job. They had no choice. But that slow, nagging, pulling feeling of not wanting to bother dragged in Matthew's middle.

"Come on," his work-mate said. "Let's get on with it."

The rigging was fixed and harnesses were fitted about their bodies. Matthew touched his harness, looked up again, and felt a clutch of fear unravel inside himself. The ropes were attached, hanging by the wall like still and solid guards. He took the rope in his hand and pulled a little, that irrational, irresistible need to check it didn't just give, would hold him, taking over everything else. Still he didn't fully trust it. Still he tried to figure in his weight and what would happen if this wasn't set up properly. His work-mate was ahead of him, scaling the wall already, looking down to see Matthew still standing there.

"Alright?" he shouted.

"Yeah," Matthew answered. "Everything's fine."

He pulled on the rope again, feeling it heavy, thick like a boa constrictor. Glad it was on his side, not trying to squeeze the life out of him. He knew fully well that rope could do that too. He made the decision to put his trust in it, staring at the rope as he began to make his way up. With each inch he moved he could feel his bond with the rope becoming stronger. Could sense that it wouldn't let him down. Could feel it working alongside him and becoming part of what he was doing. Like an animal. Like an actual living organism. He sensed its power. Which could kill or let live.

She didn't have to walk far. She slipped from the alleyway, from the narrow street, and walked in the other direction, away from where Matthew had been waiting for the van to pick him up. She felt strange dressed like this. She wondered what the people passing her would think. She felt a sadness shift in her stomach, deep down in a place she'd never felt it before. She thought she might cry, which was ridiculous, she knew, but as she rounded the bend in the road and walked upwards to the church, Kate felt a kind of sadness she was sure she'd never felt in her life.

She stood outside the church and stared up at it. The sandstone exterior reminded her of blocks of country fudge that were sold down in the little sweet shops here in Lyme Regis. The way the stone fitted together to form solid walls made her think of toffee clumping. Sticky. Sugary.

She stood outside and looked over the building for a moment. She'd already watched from across the road as everyone else went inside. She was tagging along, bringing up the rear end. She waited a second more then she stepped forward and walked through the door behind the other mourners. She sat at the back and watched. She wondered who Susie and Anthony were, the ones who'd sent the Christmas card. She guessed they must be close family. She watched the people who'd known Peter, sitting quietly and waiting. Scanned the people sitting dotted around and wondered who they might all be. She wondered if one of them was Melanie. She was the one who'd been invited, even though she never received that invitation. She was the one who should be here. But Kate looked around again. No, there weren't actually so many people, and it was only family members at the front of the church. She thought it was more likely Melanie wasn't here; she never saw the invitation anyway. She turned her attention back to the front of the church. In fact she was surprised, and relieved, that there was no one there she recognised at all. No one would know who Kate was or why she was there. No one who would know anything about Kate's life. She thought about Melanie, the person they'd actually wanted to be here. She imagined her as popular, the kind of person whose company was always desired. The kind of person you'd want as a friend. Kate thought, perhaps, just for today, she could be Melanie's friend.

The coffin was laid at the front like a kind of exhibition. Kate wondered if they were all supposed to go up at some point and have a look, parade around the dead man and peer in at him, just to make sure. But he was really dead. He was gone. Why would anyone want to look closely in on that? A couple of people at the front were crying already. Probably his wife, Kate thought, maybe a sister, maybe a daughter. Did Peter have a daughter? Kate didn't know. She thought about that. He might have had a daughter around Kate's age. Maybe they would have been friends if things were different. Maybe under other circumstances they could have been like cousins. She tried to get a better look. There was a woman with wheat-blonde hair like cooked spaghetti who was being comforted by a younger woman. On their left sat three men, no two men. Kate wasn't sure. Could be two men and one woman or three men, one with long hair. The two definite men were wearing black suits, but the third one, the indeterminate one, was wearing denim. That had to be strange for a funeral, surely, especially if you were close enough family to be sitting at the front. Kate had never wanted a brother, well, not often. Only when she needed protection. Only when the world seemed over-masculine and she could really use someone who knew how it worked. All Kate had was a useless family revolving around a useless sister. What good was that? She peered at the woman who comforted the other one. She could be Kate's sister. A proper sister. She tried to catch a clue about what she looked like, but all she could really see were the rounded backs of their shoulders, shuddering slightly with sobs.

The minister came forward from a side door somewhere and approached the congregation. To Kate's surprise he seemed to have actually known Peter. Kate had presumed this man would have been given slices of Peter's personality by the family. Little pockets in time that summed him up. Keen golfer. Liked a pint. Walked for miles with his dog through the undercliff. But instead the minister spoke of conversations he had actually had with Peter, the way he laughed, the affection he had for his wife. It was a revelation to Kate. She sat at the back of the church and saw this bundle of people all tied together by the missing man Peter, all united by his death. They were arms clasped. Shoulders connected. They were fingers lacing, hands held. They were a unit.

The vicar asked them all to take a moment quietly to remember Peter. Kate closed her eyes and bowed her head. In her mind she saw Peter, *her* Peter. She felt the swell of emotion inside of her connected to all that had happened. She had come here in the hope of finding some kind of peace, making peace. She needed to feel he would forgive her for what had happened, even though it was too late now and she couldn't ask him. She whispered lightly, too lightly for anyone to hear. *Please forgive me.* As the words left her she waited to feel her guilt lift, but instead she became aware of people ending their moment of reflection and bodies shifting in their pews and mutterings of reassurances to each other. From somewhere to her right, a couple of rows in front, she heard one woman say to another, "I see Melanie didn't come."

Shocked that anyone would be muttering like that when they were supposed to be silently paying their respects to the dead, Kate opened one eye to see who was talking. At that same moment she realised the meaning behind the words she'd heard. Melanie was not here. They looked like people from the village. The two women who seemed to know who Melanie was were obviously from the village, and they sounded sure she wasn't here. The rest of their words barely registered with Kate at all as she formulated a plan in her head.

"I should think not, all the trouble she caused."

"Hardly a surprise that she's stayed away."

Kate closed her eye again. Nobody would know. She could be Melanie's friend, and it would be like she belonged. It would feel like she was meant to be there, and somehow that made the paying of her last respects to Peter feel more genuine.

Alone, a shiver of cold running in her bones and making her teeth shudder. She stood outside the church after the service while mourners shook the hand of the calm vicar and waited in clumps for what would happen next.

Kate felt very alone and exposed. She wondered if she should just leave now while she had the chance, while no one would notice. But it was too late. Someone came up to her. A woman dressed in a smart black trouser suit. Slim, wearing heels.

"Hello there. Have you come on your own? When I saw you were standing here by yourself I assumed you must be

Anthony's girlfriend."

Kate forced a smile, a hand of panic sudden inside her. "Oh... I... er... no."

"Sorry," the woman said. "I just presumed. So how did you know Uncle Peter then?"

Kate tried to hold it all together. She had been rehearsing this: *I'm a friend of Melanie's.* But suddenly she was having doubts about saying that. How did she know Peter? Uncle Peter, the woman had said. Kate placed the woman down in her mind. His niece. Around the same age as Kate. She hadn't known he had a niece. Well, of course she didn't. Obviously she didn't.

"I knew him from work... He was such a kind person and always friendly to everyone. I just wanted to be here."

Peter's niece's face was deepening with confusion. "I thought we specifically said we didn't want anyone from his company to come..."

Kate could feel her grasp on the situation slipping even further. What *was* she doing here?

"And..." she stuttered. There was only one thing for it. "I'm a friend of Melanie's."

Peter's niece looked even more confused now. Kate saw the whole thing falling apart.

"Melanie?" said a different voice.

Someone had come up beside them. It was the lady Kate recognised from the funeral as Peter's widow. "Did you say Melanie? Is she here?" she said, accusingly.

Peter's niece faltered for a second, then turned to this other woman. "Auntie Susie," she said. "This is... sorry I didn't catch your name." She looked at Kate with just a droplet of suspicion.

"Kate," she answered. She pushed her hair behind her ear and smiled sweetly at the women.

Peter's niece turned to Susie. "Kate was just saying she worked with Peter. But didn't you request that people from the company stay away from the funeral? Surely they could have at least respected your wishes in this."

Susie closed her eyes for a second and half-whispered to

her niece. "Not now." Then she smiled at Kate again. "Kate," she said. "Thank you for coming. Are you here with Melanie?"

The woman held out her hand and Kate took it carefully.

"No," she said. "Melanie couldn't make it I'm afraid, but she wanted someone to be here… to sort of, you know, represent her."

"But Auntie Susie," said the niece. "After what happened and the way they'd treated Peter –"

Auntie Susie didn't seem too concerned. "Let's not go over it now," she said firmly. "Not today."

"Actually Melanie doesn't know I'm here…" Kate blurted out. "I mean, she was, er, like a neighbour… And I know Peter from the rope company, but I didn't know we weren't allowed to come today. I'm sorry, I'm not one of the managers or anything, I just… I wanted to come because… because I knew Peter myself. But I did know Melanie was invited."

"Really?" the niece suddenly turned on her auntie. "Why on earth…"

"For Anthony's sake, dear…" Auntie Susie said calmly. "After all, she spent a lot of time at our house and, well, she and Anthony were very close. And anyway, we must let everyone pay their respects if they want to," she said firmly. "I don't want any unpleasantness today."

She turned to Kate. "Thank you for taking the trouble to come. Of course I wouldn't want you to have felt you were not allowed to come, since you did know Peter yourself, after all. Now you will come along to the cemetery now, won't you? And after, back to our house, of course, you're most welcome."

Kate smiled, a warm feeling moving inside her. "Thank you," she said. "I'd like that."

"Have you met Anthony?" Auntie Susie asked.

"Actually, no, I've only heard of him… I mean, I've just heard his name, really."

"Well I'll make sure I introduce you when you come back to the house."

The house was like no other Kate had ever been in. She walked with the clutch of mourners up to the top of the street and crossed the road. They came to a gravel path held by trees on either side and after a couple of minutes the trees cleared to reveal a massive garden and a house. To the right of the house a semicircular driveway enclosed a jeep and a yellow convertible. Just like the kind of house she always imagined Matthew to be in, paint brush in his hand, envy in his eyes. Kate tried to act as if this was all normal to her. Had seen houses like this hundreds of times. Had stood by cars like these on dozens of occasions. Had been with people to whom this was all commonplace.

She was planted for a moment on the gravel path that would run to the right into the gravel drive, up under the wheels of those cars. She was staring at the big, apple-green garden and the old converted farmhouse. Then she realised people were going into the house. She caught Auntie Susie's smile and the niece's look of suspicion still fixed in the air, buzzing like an electrical wire. Kate took a breath. This was normal. It was completely normal. She stepped forward and followed them into the house.

She moved slow inside. This is where he lived. This is the space he used to inhabit when he was alive. She looked around to try and catch something that was his or was handled by him, used by him. She searched for things, solid things that still held his fingerprints, his DNA, tiny traces of his life that meant, in some small part, he still existed. Dog lead hanging on a hook by the door. Golf clubs bundled into the cupboard under the stairs. Semicircles worn into the stair carpet where his heavy feet had trod time after time.

He was standing there before she knew what was happening to her. Pale-blue jeans covered a pair of long legs, his long hair reached his shoulders and a beard covered the bottom half of his face. The niece moved up to Kate's side and followed her eyes.

"Oh, that's Anthony," she said. "My cousin." She dropped her voice and tilted her head towards Kate's ear. "I know what you're thinking," she said. "But don't mind him, he always looks like that, but I'm sure if you know Melanie you understand. I expect Auntie Susie did her best to get him to wear a suit, but…" she shrugged, then held her head upwards and called to him. "Anthony!" He looked up. Pool-blue eyes, a little lazy, glanced in the niece's direction. He looked as if he'd stumbled into the wrong house. He looked like nobody else there. He looked like a missing person. Displaced. A ghost.

"This is Kate," The niece said. "She's friends with *Melanie."*

Kate felt the edge in the way she had said the other woman's name.

Anthony was trying too hard to not react. He put out his hand and Kate placed hers in it. Surely she wasn't meant to shake hands, was she? They stood there for a second stupidly holding hands, neither of them sure of what to do. Then Anthony dropped her fingers and said, "How do you know Melanie?"

"Well, it's funny really," Kate said. "But I live in the flat where she used to live, down in the town, and we just sort of hit it off and stayed friends."

It was a ridiculous thing to say. It was out of her mouth before she knew what she was doing.

"And you work with her, of course," the niece said. "You're from the same company, aren't you?"

Kate looked at her, her mouth slightly open, words dashing into sentences in her head. We met over the particulars of the flat. We became friends when I passed on her mail to her. She had to say something, and she knew the truth wouldn't cover it.

"Well, I met her because of the flat... when I moved in."

"Oh right," Anthony said. "So she's still in Dorset?"

Kate felt around in the lies.

"Where is she living now?" Anthony went on. "I thought maybe she'd moved… away." his words dropped from him as if he'd let go of the leash they were connected to, too tired to hold them anymore.

The niece looked awkwardly around, trying to fill the empty space that circled between them now.

"Come on, I'm sure we don't want to talk about this right now," the niece said. "Melanie's not here, is she, so… let's just leave it at that."

Kate looked at her feet. "No," she answered. Then she looked up again. She saw Anthony's face being followed by a dim blush and the niece looking anywhere but at him. Kate flicked a switch inside herself and tried to change the subject. She looked up into the niece's face. "Is it OK me being here? I mean, I didn't mean to intrude or anything, and I didn't realise no one was supposed to come... from the factory."

"If Auntie Susie doesn't mind..." the niece shrugged. "And if you didn't know, it's not your fault, no harm done. Anyway I haven't noticed anybody *did* come... I mean anyone else."

*

Anthony sat on the edge of his bed in his bedroom, the same room he'd had almost all his life. Apparently his parents had lived in a small semi on the outskirts of Lyme when Anthony was just a baby, but with them already having two boys before him and the prospect of big bikes and football gear looming in their future, they'd moved here to this house. Anthony's dad was doing well at work then, and houses were cheaper.

He sat now, an hour after the last person had said how sorry they were and left the wake in the house, and he wondered what his dad would make of all this. He wondered if his dad had thought about what it would be like without him, if he'd imagined the funeral and what people would say and how life would go on.

Anthony's brothers and their wives had been laughing about something earlier, right here in the house, just a few hours after they'd buried Peter. They'd actually been laughing. Having a joke about who knows what, Anthony didn't want to know, he didn't want to hear whatever it was they'd found so funny. But they'd been laughing. In this house. Today. Anthony didn't feel like he'd ever laugh again, and he certainly couldn't have mustered a giggle today, at a wake for God's sake, at their own father's wake. But Anthony's brothers didn't seem to have hung onto it all likc Anthony did. They seemed to have achieved a distance already. At least that was how it appeared to Anthony.

He felt his fingers grip around the edge of the bed he sat on. He couldn't imagine a time when he'd be able to put it behind him, or even put it aside for enough time to have a laugh about something else. He couldn't see how he would ever get over this. Like his brothers would. Maybe even his mother, maybe it would even be easier for her than it would be for Anthony. After all, she had nothing to blame herself about. Of course she said she did, obviously she thought right now that maybe she could have done something. But she couldn't. Anthony knew that. And the feeling she had right now would pass. For her. For his brothers. For everyone else. But not for Anthony. Because he knew it. He knew deep down in his heart that, no matter what anyone said, no matter what relatives and neighbours and doctors and counsellors said, he really was to blame.

*

The plane journey from Portugal back to England was giving Melanie too much time to think. That was never a good thing. Cabin crew came down the aisle with the trolley and Melanie leaned over and asked for a gin and tonic. She didn't care what time it was. She couldn't sit here for the next two hours and let her mind keep going over things.

She took the little plastic cup, poured the tonic from the little metal can, and looked out of the window.

It was only last week that she'd flown to Portugal in the first place. She'd managed to go to her new job on Monday, Tuesday, and Wednesday, but by then it was already unbearable.

She hadn't even had time to find a flat out there to call home, unpack her things, or explore her new surroundings. No time to make friends and settle into her new life away from all this, before she was back. She definitely wasn't staying for long, but it had to be done. Unfinished business.

Melanie had to leave England when she did. She hadn't been forced to or told to, but she knew she had to leave. And she had to leave quick. She tried to tell herself she'd done nothing wrong, but it was in every turn of her head, every blink of her eyes, every tiny, un-thought-through movement she made. She couldn't stay there. She wouldn't be able to live with herself if she did. Her boss had already mentioned to her the idea of a transfer to Portugal so she went to see him. He had nodded, his hands clasped on the desk, his body hunched forward, his eyes filling with borrowed, momentary sorrow. He said he understood. Said he could imagine how she must feel. At a time like this. In the circumstances. Melanie had kept quiet and kept her emotions under control and thought to herself, he doesn't understand at all, this man, he can't possibly imagine how she feels. She couldn't look at the office, the car park, the stair, the kitchen, the building at all without thinking about it and feeling it and being crushed by the overwhelming guilt. The feeling that she had to leave right now.

*

Kate first met Matthew one evening when the sun had just left the sky and the pubs were filling with tourists. She'd gone to the pub with an old school friend who was back in town for a cousin's wedding. Something like that, though Kate didn't pay that much attention to the details. She'd been invited out for a drink and she went. Anything to get out of the house. Anything to leave her childhood home which she now felt she'd come to the end of her time with. Outgrown. Outlived. And she could hardly stand being there anymore. Kate could feel herself mentally leaving. The house would be like a layer of skin that she could shake off to grow something new instead. All she needed now was a place to go. As she walked down to the pub that evening, she stopped for a second at the bottom of Silver Street and looked up the road. She couldn't see it from here, but she knew right at the top of the street, where the main road sliced through, just on the hill, was the sign *Welcome to Devon.* It signalled an invisible border. A full stop to her county, another opening up on the other side of that hill. She'd sometimes thought, as a girl, how different it must be over there, in Devon. Another county. Maybe she should try a city. Bristol. Southampton. Life would be different there.

And then she met Matthew.

Matthew entered the pub that night like a dream into her sleeping brain. It was a moment she would never forget. She was standing with her old school friend, talking about nothing in particular, when he walked in, carrying gifts in his arms. And it was like he'd been sent especially for her.

Kate never usually went down to this pub, The Bay Hotel: it was right by the sea and attracted tourists, and she could only presume that was why she'd never seen Matthew before.

But her old school friend wanted to come here tonight. She said she wanted to smell the sea while she drank cocktails, wanted to feel the breeze rush in every time someone opened the door to leave or enter. She said she wanted to get as much of her old life by the ocean as she could while she was here. And Kate said OK.

She'd often think, after, how strange it is the way things move. If she hadn't gone out that night, if her old friend hadn't felt the pull of the water, if she hadn't had the courage to stare at him and then smile when he looked back. If it hadn't been his work-mate's birthday. Maybe they would never have met.

And it was exactly the right time in her life for her to meet someone.

*

The first time Melanie's boss had called her into his office to mention the transfer, she was sure something was wrong. It seemed silly now, that childish nervousness that overcomes you when the boss says, 'Can you come up to the office for a minute please?'

She hadn't been in the job long, but she was working hard at it to prove herself and thought she was doing all right. Even so, the thoughts immediately started scurrying around in her head.

Did I make a big mistake and haven't realised?

Does he hate me?

Am I too slow at my work?

Is he going to fire me right now?

But it was nothing like that. It was about Portugal. He

was pushing an idea across the desk at her. She'd sat there and he'd said, "How would you feel about moving?"

"Moving?" she said. "Where to? How long for? Why?" It could still be a bad thing. Maybe it was because he wanted to get rid of her after all. Maybe he couldn't fire her. Maybe moving her was his only option.

"Our factory in Portugal," he said. "We're sending a few people over, show 'em how it's done out there, or at least that's the idea."

She didn't say anything, but just stared at him over the desk. Portugal? He wanted her to go to Portugal?

He pointed at her. "You're the first person I thought of," he said. "I know you're ambitious, Mel, and this is a great opportunity for you."

She was still staring at him. Portugal?

"I... er... I don't know. I'd need to think about it. I mean, you're right, I really do want to make something of my career, go places... it's just... Portugal is going a bit further than I had in mind."

He smiled then and leaned back in his chair. "Of course," he said. "Sleep on it, of course, but don't think about it too long, I need to send someone out there soon."

She'd thought about it. But she couldn't go. She was just settling into the job she had. Needed to prove to everyone around her that she could do it, that she was the right person for the job. But then everything changed.

Peter died.

*

Anthony had stayed in his room for a while. There was nothing to do in this space of time after the wake. His thoughts were making his body tense to the point of shaking and he could feel the consuming grief pulling at him again and again. In the end he got up and went downstairs. His mother was in the kitchen piling dishes on the worktop ready to be washed. She stacked the plates in the dishwasher and left a wooden chopping board and the good crockery on the side to be washed by hand.

Anthony leaned against the door frame and watched her for a second, his hands grasping at their opposite elbows.

She turned.

"I'll do that," he said.

"Are you sure?"

He stood up straight and moved towards her. "Yeah, you go and have a rest."

She ran her hand through her hair and sighed deeply. "Well, if you're sure you don't mind, it has been a long day."

Anthony forced a smile and motioned for his mother to go. He ran hot water into the sink and watched as washing up liquid made perfect shiny bubbles. It was hard to imagine how this was going to work. How day to day life would be now. It was hard to imagine how life would be now at all. Somehow, he and his mother would have to find a way to live here, the two of them, together.

He looked up, to the window and the back garden beyond it. The washing line stretched out like a power cable above the grass, not used for months over the winter, but always there. He wondered if that's what it would be like. If his dad would always be here in one way or another. The rope, that formed the bones of Peter's life, was everywhere. Anthony wondered if he'd ever stop noticing it. Memories seemed to attach themselves to everything he looked at. Things he hadn't thought of in years seemed to resurface at the mere glance to a photo in a frame on the sideboard, the space by the door where his boots used to be, a small dog in the street, the length of very thin rope that he had brought back from his factory: still strung across the back garden waiting for washing.

*

The rope burned if he swung on it for too long. He could feel it shift against his skin, tight, in the palms of his hands, the whole weight of his body depending on it. He lifted his knees together, up to meet his middle and he held on tight as he grasped the rope and let it take him.

He was aged about twelve at the time, and Anthony remembered the feel of that rope and the feel of his body free in the air over the ditch for all his life. He would go there at lunch time or after school with a friend, but it wasn't the friends he remembered, they all turned out to be false anyway, it was the feeling of being free, perhaps the only time he ever really had it, swinging across the ditch over the road from school, the pull of his body and the rope above him, secure on the strong branches of a tree. It was a sense of security that only the rope could give him. The rope that he'd tried so hard to reject when he got older. Because his dad wanted him to love it like he did. Because his dad wanted him to follow the family line and conform, as Anthony saw it.

*

He took the first few cups from the worktop and let them fall into the hot soapy water. He watched as his own hands turned inside them and brought them out clean. His dad had drunk from these cups. His dad had stood right here and done just what Anthony was doing right now.

Anthony couldn't imagine how any of these things could be laid aside and forgotten. Or how all the small physical things with a connection to Peter could ever be looked at or touched without the draining feeling of loss and regret pulling his body to the ground.

*

He would make the arrangements, he said. He would tell them she was moving to Portugal straight away.

So she'd gone to Portugal and the company had fixed up a hotel for her for a week. It was comfortable. And they would be able to find an apartment for her after that.

But it was lonely. And it was too far away from all that had happened.

She'd gone. But the feelings and the guilt had gone with her. After all, she knew she was the one to blame. The whole sequence of events had been her fault. No one else. If anything, it got worse. She knew no one would ever be able to convince her otherwise. The further away she was from the scene of what had happened, the worse she felt. She hadn't been able to concentrate on anything at all on the Monday in her new job. Somehow, she had to get forgiveness for what she'd done. Some kind of *closure*, somehow. So she came back. Here she was on a flight back to England already. She could have worked through until Friday and then come back for Christmas but she took annual leave and came straight back on the Thursday. It really was true what they said, you can't run away from problems, especially not a problem like this one. You only take it with you, and out there, in a foreign country, on her own, it seemed to multiply. The night time was the worst. When she closed her eyes all she could see was Peter.

Deep in the Portuguese night, feeble motorbikes troubling the streets outside and the moon like a Christmas light, Melanie decided there was only one way to deal with this. The question was, how? There was only one person in the family back in Lyme who could possibly want to see her face again. But unfortunately that was the one person Melanie wanted to see least of all.

*

It was the Friday following the funeral. Kate was walking up Silver Street with her black cloth bag over her shoulder. Denim jacket on. Christmas lights hung in semi-hoops from building to building, shop to shop, like untied daisy chains. She felt the damp ground beneath her seep a little into her worn shoes as she reached the top of the street. She stopped for a moment at the edge of the hill. She looked back once and saw the curve in the road, the Indian restaurant, charity shop, the bulge of a building hiding the library from her on the other side of the road. Down towards the sea cars moved slow on the wet tarmac, a woman wearing a green mac carrying shopping bags walked with her head down against the wind, Christmas trees sparkled in windows. Kate wondered about what it felt like to have lost someone this close to Christmas. She wondered how you were supposed to cope, carry on, sing carols, open presents, pretend to be happy. She wondered if people expected that. She turned back towards the top of the hill and the road that sliced the head of Lyme and carried cars to Devon. She walked on, crossed the road and reached the bottom of the long dirt-track drive. She wondered what she was supposed to say.

*

Inside the house Susie made tea. Kate had thought Susie would be the kind of woman who would have a teapot, silver or maybe Royal Doulton, and she would use real tea leaves and a silver tea strainer which she would hold steadily over each ornate little teacup as she poured. But she didn't. Susie disappeared into the kitchen for five minutes and then came back carrying two mugs, plain blue, no fuss. She sat down, setting the two mugs on a low table and then she held her hand to her forehead as if she had a migraine and said, "Oh, I'm so sorry, do you have sugar? I forgot the sugar."

Kate was surprised at how delicate she seemed, after all, in the note in the Christmas card she had stated they were all doing fine.

"No, that's OK," Kate said. "I don't have sugar."

A silence settled in the room for a moment and Kate began to feel uncomfortable. She looked around, caught the eye of people in photos on a sideboard. A woman, in black and white, standing outside a cottage with five kids huddled round her legs, Susie and Peter on a boat somewhere, sun bled in their skin, the three sons when they were young, shuffling on a sofa, grandkids as they are now, Anthony. She shook them off and looked back at Susie. "I just thought…" she began. "Well, I just wondered, wanted to say, if there's anything you need, you know, anything I can do."

Susie forced a smile, but it held more pain than any smile Kate had ever seen, and Kate realised she'd probably heard those exact words a hundred times already. She let her sentence trail. "Anything at all," she said. She felt stupid for offering now. Of course Susie didn't need her for anything. She had family, a niece, sons and their wives and their kids who probably took her mind off the whole thing when they were around. And Anthony, the quiet one, her other son, who wore jeans to the funeral, on his own, most likely still living here, consoling her, doing all the things she might need doing, fetching all the things she might need.

Susie looked to the floor. Kate watched her and saw a harsh swallow, a tremble in her skin and a moment where her breathing came out like gulps in water. Kate could see her set her teeth and close her eyes as if there was too much noise. Then she breathed out slowly, composing herself, supressing tears and sudden shaking in her hands. She looked up, straight at Kate. "That's very thoughtful of you," Susie said, "but I wouldn't want to trouble you."

"Oh it would be no trouble."

Kate quickly retracted as soon as the words were out. She'd said them too eagerly. She could see Susie's face falter again, a wariness and a need to distance herself heavy around her mouth and in her jaw. Kate had looked at her for too long. She was sure Susie could feel it, but Kate couldn't stop. She wanted to know how it felt. She wanted to see some sort of evidence on Susie's face, in her eyes, clear on her skin. How had it been when he was alive? How did they live? What happened in the spare moments that were left over when their kids had grown and gone and no one else was here? What was he like, Peter, when he lived in this house? Did he still hold his wife when he was old? Kiss her, touch her, did he always love her? Or did it pass and move on like weather?

A silence blanketed them again. Then Kate looked around at the tidy room, the plain beige walls, the long, loosely draped curtains. "Is your Christmas tree in another room?" she asked.

Susie swallowed again and made an effort to clear her throat of emotion. "No," she answered. And for a second Kate thought that's all she would say. Then she frowned and the difficulties of grief at this time of year travelled over her face. "I don't think we'll have Christmas this year," she went on. "At least not in this house." She took a sip of her tea and focussed her gaze on the corner of the low coffee table, as if looking at Kate made speaking this harder, as if another person's face, *any* person's face, with their worry-less lives and their inability to understand, might make Susie's composure crumble and her resolve break. She spoke slowly at first, and then seemed to keep going like she couldn't stop. "My other two sons, and their families..." she said. "Of course it's all for children anyway, isn't it, they asked us, but I don't know, I don't think it would be fair of me to inflict myself on them this year. They'd be better without me, I'd only ruin the atmosphere and I don't want to do that, not for the children."

She stopped suddenly and Kate thought she was about to cry. She saw the tears flicker in the corners of Susie's mouth as she stopped speaking, shook her head a little, and looked down again. Kate hadn't expected that. She sat opposite this woman, newly widowed, and she thought how she had been fooled by the way she had held it together at the funeral and the words in the note in the Christmas card. *All fine. Doing fine. Coping fine.* She felt like a fool for believing it, like she'd been tricked, when all the time Susie was every bit the widow, every bit broken and full of despair. She wondered about all the ways Susie covered up, all the pretence and appearances. She thought about the children, the things in the note last year about the summer they'd spent, the holidays, the barbecues in the back garden, the sense of fun and happiness laid with each mark of the pen on the paper. Was any of it true?

"So, it will be me and Anthony this year," Susie went on, a firm nod of her head to show this was a decision she'd made. "And I don't think we will really have Christmas."

Kate waited for a moment, trying to figure this woman and her place amidst her grief. "Of course, I'm sorry," Kate said at last.

An awkwardness passed and Susie held her mug to her face. She took a sip of tea and then changed the subject quickly. "Do you hear from Melanie often?" she asked.

"Not so much, no."

"Hmm, I suppose she's busy."

"Yes," Kate answered. "She's ... busy."

"But you worked with her, at the factory? Is that right?"

She hesitated as she considered the truth. What did truth matter anyway, in a situation like this? What did details really matter?

"Yes, that's right," she said.

"It must have been a terrible shock for you all."

Kate looked up, into Susie's eyes. No one had said this yet, not really. No one had considered how other people had been affected. "It was," Kate said. She motioned towards Susie. "I mean, it doesn't compare, I know, but I have found it hard. In fact... I haven't been back to work since."

Susie kept her eyes held right there. "Really?" she said.

"Yeah, the doctor signed me off, stress, you know, I just can't stop thinking about it."

*

It was a relief at first, when the niece was at the door, knocking lightly and peering through the glass. Susie put her mug down and got up to let her in. They hugged carefully and kissed each other on the cheek. Kate tried not to stare. Nobody in her family did things like that.

"You remember Kate," Susie was saying. "Friend of Melanie's."

The niece walked forward. "Oh yes," she said. "Of course."

There was something sticking to the back of her words. *Of course.* She hadn't believed it in the first place, that day, at the funeral, she was the one who could see right through Kate. *Melanie? As if Melanie would have a friend. A friend like you.* Kate knew what she was thinking. It was all too unlikely. Too neat. It wasn't true.

She turned to Susie. "Actually I was just popping in, Auntie Su, to see if you needed anything, but if I'd known you had company..."

Kate imagined Susie being bombarded by people popping in to see if she needed anything. Thought she could hear the sigh in Susie as soon as the words were spoken again. What could she possibly need right now that anyone could bring her?

"No, it's fine," Susie said. Then something seemed to switch on in her head and she forced another one of her brilliant, deceitful smiles. "Actually, yes, why don't you two call down to the village for me, pick me up one or two things while you're there."

Kate and the niece glanced at each other. Either she wanted rid of them both, or she was seeing the bud of a possible friendship and pushing it into the sun. Kate thought she wanted rid of them both. She wanted rid of everyone at the moment. And Kate understood that. Better than the pretence and the flashed smiles and the word *coping* in the note in the Christmas card, better than any of the cover-ups, Kate understood that.

They didn't say a word as they walked. Gravel crunching under their feet, the cold white sky above them becoming shaded by trees as they walked away from the house and down the long drive. They made it to the bottom of the drive and then crossed the road, Kate trying to smile as they rushed to avoid a car powering over the hill from Devon. They walked down, past the Indian restaurant, the library on the other side. They still hadn't spoken, until they approached The Volunteer with its exterior squashed between other doorways, the misplaced sign declaring it to be an Irish pub even though everyone here knew it wasn't, knew it never would be no matter what signs said and what beers it decided to stock.

"That's where our Anthony will be," the niece said.

Kate turned sharply to take in her face while she spoke.

"Every Sunday without fail since… Probably weekdays as well as far as I know."

Kate tried to imagine the man in denim sitting inside on his own, holding his pint, stooped over a table like he was old. "You mean after work?" she asked. "He goes in there every day after work?"

The niece huffed. "Anthony doesn't work, not anymore.

All Anthony does as far as I can see these days is get in everyone's way. He's been no use to Auntie Susie at all. All he does is drink." She aimed her head at the pub door. "Sit in there, and then wander around the town like a lost bloody dog. As if nobody else suffers. As if he's the only one affected." She glanced again at the window of The Volunteer and then moved on. "And you can tell that to Melanie," she said. "When you speak to her."

They went together to the bakery and bought the cakes Susie had asked for. It seemed obvious to Kate that this errand was a sham. They bought the cakes and then stood up on the path, beside the huge Christmas tree that was planted for the duration of the holidays by the side of the road, and they both tried to summon up some sort of way to end this. It was almost painful it was so awkward. The niece could smell the lies, Kate was sure of it.

They stood together for a minute. The niece was looking out to the sea, cold wind fingering her hair, then she said, "I go to the grave. It's so sad. It's not like we were that close or anything, but it's just so sad. Sometimes I go and see the flowers and the cards and the things people have written, and it's so very sad."

Kate waited. She hoped this woman wasn't going to cry, but there didn't seem to be any tears in her voice, so Kate just waited. Then the niece turned to look at her and seemed to be testing her. "I might go there now actually. You want to come?"

*

The church is high in the afternoon air as they stand at its doorway. That funeral is the only one time Kate has ever been inside. Doubts she'll be going in many more times either. They only pause there for a second before the niece is moving on towards the grave and Kate is following her. They tread carefully between graves and the grass outlines of coffins six feet down, slight mounds in the earth still showing where bodies lie. They make sure they don't touch any headstones, as if contact will wake sleeping souls or invite spirits into their lives. The niece stops and crouches by the right grave. Kate still stands, gazing down at the headstone, flowers propped up at the edges, photos laid by its side, one of him probably not so long before he died, one when he was young, in his twenties, with long hair draped on his shoulders. Kate stares. His physical features, his eyes, his mouth, his hair, all passed on to today, all walking around the town still, drinking in the pub, wandering the streets. Anthony. She forces her eyes away from the picture, sees pages with poems and messages strewn before it like playing cards thrown in on a table top. The niece leans forward and picks one up, looks at it, then hands it up to Kate: *Uncle Peter, we all miss you so much, can't believe you've left us, but you are at peace now xx* Kate hands it back and the niece passes her another: *Grandpa, why did you have to go? We miss you xx* There are at least twenty more of these, but as the niece tries to force another to Kate's fingers, Kate bats it away, puts her hand to her cheek and turns her head to the side.

The niece stands up. "Why are you crying?" she asks. "You hardly knew him, did you?"

*

Peter's grandfather twisted the rope in his hands fast. He pulled it taut and watched as it shuddered, waited for it to stop and hold still so he could carry on his work. The rope complied.

"You can trust rope," his grandfather said, as Peter sat on the ground, fascinated by what the old man was doing. "It won't let you down. See. Not like people."

Peter glanced at his grandfather's face and saw a second of sadness. The old man knew the boy's eyes were on him, and that he probably shouldn't have said that. But everyone has to learn it sometime. Everyone has to grow up.

*

She thought about Susie in the house in Uplyme. She thought about a normal day, just another day, the quiet wrapped around her, the hours never-ending, moving forward towards nothing.

She wondered if it was just the two of them, Susie and Anthony, both trying not to catch the eye of the dead man in the photos on the sideboard, both trying not to look at each other, or anywhere that might require them to speak of anything that mattered at all. Kate thought Christmas was a nonsense. Just a silly invented day. When it was stripped back and revealed for what it really was, when it was laid bare and seen to be as stark as every other day, it was disappointingly ordinary.

*

Rain moved almost horizontally in the air, a strong sea wind carrying it like arrows. The force took the rain through the streets where it appeared at windows like the tapping of ghosts. Then, before it could get comfortable and slow, the wind took the rain again and moved it on to Devon.

Kate had woken to the sound of the weather. She'd moved her small body beside Matthew in the bed, and she'd thought about the leaky window frames and the wetness that would seep in, the wind that would find its way through gaps like sunlight through a hole in a fence. Sometimes she would pass by one of the windows and she would feel a gentle blow of cool air. She would hold her hand out to feel it, a constant stream of air, as if the house was breathing on her, one long breath. And she wanted it to stop. She wanted the double glazing, the clean plastic and the tight seals that didn't collect black gunk in their corners. She wanted some peace.

She'd tried to stop herself from thinking about it, but it was a niggle in her brain, a thread she'd started to pull, and now she couldn't stop. She'd got out of bed that morning with January facing her and she knew she'd not be able to look a new year in the eyes till she followed this to its end.

She only had two things, two buildings, the house in Uplyme and The Volunteer, to tie her thoughts of him to his physical body. Two places she knew for sure he might be. She practised in the kitchen in the morning the face she would make when she saw him. The surprised expression. The smile. She made the face again and again and Matthew almost caught her as he wandered in, T-shirt and boxers crumpled on his body. She must have jumped. "What you doing?" he asked.

"Nothing." And she turned away and pretended to straighten mugs in the cupboard.

Matthew yawned and moved alongside her to reach for one of the mugs. She watched his mouth expand with sleep still caught in his breath. He had a chubby face. He wasn't fat or anything, but his cheeks bulged slightly, naturally, like a frog or a desperate hamster.

"Did it all go OK at the shopping centre in the end?" she asked. "You got it finished in time for them opening up again?"

"Yeah," he answered. "No problem. Got a short job on Friday, but then starting another big one on Saturday."

He shunted on his feet in the kitchen now so that he was behind Kate. Reached his arms around her middle and brought his head down to her neck. "Let's go back to bed," he whispered.

She squirmed a little in his grasp. "I'm dressed," she said.

He burrowed his face into her neck a little more. "So?" he said. "We can soon change that."

She leaned herself away from him. "You have to go to work."

He straightened up and loosened his arms around her. Could see he wasn't getting anywhere. He sighed and let go of her. "Yeah, fine," he said.

She watched him while he boiled the kettle and stared out of the window.

Half an hour later she had left the flat. She touched the cold walls as she went down the dark staircase and opened the door at the bottom into the little alleyway. Stray tourists wobbled along the narrow path, one foot on the road until a van shunted along behind them and they leapt into shop doorways. Kate held her bag tightly under her arm. You never knew who any of these people might be. She turned the corner, glanced at the sea, and then made her way up the street.

*

It was only a few days ago that Melanie had left Dorset with a single suitcase trailing her feet on the pavement. She'd gone without saying goodbye to anyone. As soon as it had happened. She just got on the first flight she could.

And she was back already. She looked at the clock on the kitchen wall. 10.37 am. In Uplyme Anthony would still be sleeping. Susie would be awake, grief still so infectious it ran riot through her body spider-like. Melanie looked out of the window, imagining the quiet house in Uplyme, dust and the memories of what had happened swirling in the light creeping through curtains that stayed drawn all day long.

*

They all hated Anthony. He was an outcast in his own family. His mother would always love him. She told him so. And he had to believe her. But his brothers and his cousins, even his aunt and uncles, they all looked at him like he was a piece of shit these days. People kept dropping in with bunches of flowers and sympathy cards. Looking at him and his clothes and his bearded face with something like suspicion. The neighbours kept asking him how his mother was and then looking at him like there was more he should be doing. Like he wasn't enough. Like he didn't measure up.

He left the house. Couldn't face anyone. The feeling was getting worse every day. Guilt. Sadness. Anxiety. He positioned his body against it. He had his hands jammed into the tight pockets on his jeans. Shoulders hunched a bit. Head tilted down. Eyes peering out from under his fringe. If he didn't look people fully in the face he wouldn't have to see what was in their eyes. If he didn't stand up straight when he walked they might not see him at all.

He rounded the corner at the bottom of the gravel path quickly, just in case any of the neighbours saw him and wanted to ask how he was, how his mother was, or tell him how sorry they were. He couldn't stand much more of that. He glanced around, but there was no sign of any of them.

He has long legs. His hands are rammed right down in his pockets when he comes round the corner. He looks up from under his fringe. His hair, shorter around his face and long on his back, is the colour of wild nuts. Chestnut, she thinks. He is obviously hiding from something. The bottom half of his face is protected by a beard and a long moustache and his eyes are only just poking out from beneath his hair. He walks quickly. Doesn't notice Kate at all. She gets up from the bus shelter she has been sitting in as he passes and she follows him along the street.

She could still make it seem like a coincidence, she thought. She can still disguise this with accident. Bump into him in a shop. Reach for the same item at exactly the same time. Create a situation.

She followed him down the street, watching the way he walked. His hair forced on to his shoulders by the collar of his jacket. His legs elongated by the tight stonewash he was wearing. She looked down at her own clothes and wondered if she was up to scratch. She was wearing a denim jacket, below that a black gypsy skirt clung to her hips and then trailed down to the floor. She placed herself next to him in her mind and thought they would look good together.

Anthony reached the bottom of the street. He stopped and glanced up the road to check for traffic, but if he saw Kate he made no sign that he had. He ran slightly as he crossed the road, just outside the Red Lion pub, then he headed for the steps at the bottom that would take him towards the sea. The oversized Christmas tree stood in a parking bay by the curve in the road, like it did every year. Anthony paid it no attention, so used to seeing it. Only the tourists reacted at the sight of this fully trimmed up spectacle taking the place of a saloon or a 4x4.

Kate was doing her best to keep up, trying to work out all the time what she would say if she came face to face with him. *What a surprise. I wasn't following you, no.* She crossed the road and ran down the steps. She could just see him to the right heading for the cobbled pebble beach. She was rushing so as not to lose him. Anthony was stepping onto the pebbles, hands in his pockets again. He walked towards the water and Kate walked cautiously onto the beach, her feet balancing and skidding on pebble after pebble. She watched her feet for a second as she tried to move forward on the rocks. When she looked up again she could see him just standing there, his back to her, his head held up for the first time since he'd rounded the corner at the bottom of his own drive, staring out at the sea.

Kate felt the salted air fill her lungs, cold, like the wind swirled inside her now as she took a chunk of breath in through her mouth and nose, held for a moment, then sighed it out. She walked straight up to him. Now or never. Just do it.

She touched his arm, below his inner elbow where it bent to allow his hands into the small pockets of his denim jacket. She looked up into his face and felt a slap in her chest when his eyes, blue like sky, rested on her face.

"Hi," she said. For a second he just looked at her. She could see a pebble of confusion make its way to the surface, his mouth moving just enough to show he didn't know what to say, what to do.

"We met at the funeral," she went on. "Peter's funeral... I mean, your dad."

"Oh yeah," he said, but Kate wasn't sure if he really remembered her at all.

"I'm Kate," she said. "Friend of Melanie's."

She saw the same hidden panic flood his face at the mention of Melanie's name again. He was nodding, looking down at the ground again. "Yeah, yeah, well, I'm Anthony," he said.

Now or never. Just do it.

"Hey listen," Kate said. "Do you fancy getting a coffee or something?" She aimed her thumb over her shoulder in the direction of the shops and cafes. "It's bloody freezing down here."

He looked stunned for a moment, then he said OK and Kate felt relief spread in her body.

They turned and faced the town again, away from the sea. They rounded the little stone staircase and made their way up, around the back of the road, and nipped into the tearooms that nestle in the wall there. Limp tinsel was strung over old paintings and a length of fairy lights criss-crossed the front window of the teashop.

They ordered coffee and Kate watched as Anthony nervously used his fingers as drumsticks on the edge of the table, changing the rhythm with every moment that passed and sometimes rubbing a single finger along the edge of the table as if he were wiping it clean.

"So... sorry," he said. "How do you know Melanie?"

"Oh, that, well, I live in the flat she used to live in, and..." she shrugged. "Yeah, that's it."

"Oh, right. So that's why I've never heard her talk about you," he said slowly. "She's never even been in touch since she moved out of that flat." He seemed distracted for a moment and Kate saw a small sigh escape him. "So, you see her much?"

She shrugged again. "Now and then, you know."

Anthony looked down at his lap. The index finger of one hand continued to slowly rub the edge of the table. Kate could see his blue eyes below his eyelashes and his mouth below his beard.

"She mention me?" he asked quietly.

She could feel the weight of the question. What did he want?

"Well..." she answered. "Why do you ask?"

He looked up quickly then, his body relaxing and leaning back in his chair, his arms outstretched, hands still at the table. "I just wondered," he said. "She probably told you what a loser I am."

He laughed. But Kate knew it wasn't funny.

"Why would you say that?" she asked.

He looked down again. "I... you know what it's like, I don't fit in with my family. Surely Melanie told you something like that. If not about me then in general, or... I mean about herself and... I mean you must know that if you know Melanie.

She was always saying we were loners... that people didn't understand us, that our families didn't get us, that we didn't fit in. Me and her were the same like that." He hesitated. "Or maybe she didn't talk about me at all…?"

Kate waited for his words to settle. He was looking at her face now as if, if he looked hard enough, he'd get what he wanted. The answers would seep out. She lifted the coffee cup up to her face. She took a sip and then lowered it again. "She didn't talk about it much, no."

Anthony looked surprised, or disappointed, or both. "She usually likes to tell everybody about that, about being some kind of outcast in her own family," he said. "She seems to think it makes her more *different.*"

"People are never as different as they think they are," Kate said.

She saw him give a genuine smile for the first time, and felt herself relax. He'd found something he hadn't expected. Some kind of allegiance. Some kind of empathy.

"So," she said. "How are you anyway?"

A slight blush. First to his skin, then to hers.

"How am I? What do you mean by that?"

"Sorry, I don't mean to pry," she said. "Just, you know, with your dad and everything."

"Oh right, yeah," he shrugged. "Well, I'm OK, you know, as well as can be expected." He leaned forward as he said it, his eyes a little wider, his face a little more intent, an exaggerated expression.

"Of course, sorry, it was a stupid question."

"No, not a stupid question, just, you know, what can I say? There's no real answer, is there, I mean, not a real answer."

She could feel the urge to come clean and tell him everything pushing inside her. The danger of it pulled her back from the lies she'd told and how he'd take it stopped her. But still, that need to share everything with him, the one person who might understand, was impossible to deny completely.

She looked at him.

"But, you know… it's not as if you didn't fit in the

family, is it? You don't really think that do you? I mean, you know, you look… I mean…" Kate could feel her words stop in the air between herself and Anthony. "Don't you feel like you look like your dad?"

This one really was a stupid question. For a moment she wanted to take it back. Wished she could. But then again she just wanted to hear him say it, *Yeah, everyone says I look like him.* She could already see so much of Peter in Anthony but somehow she thought it would help her feel Peter's face through Anthony's if he said it. Help her see his eyes. Know the dead man now through his son. Anthony didn't answer. He looked away instead, out of the window.

Kate said, "I suppose we all look like our parents anyway, don't we? At least a bit. I suppose we just can't see it ourselves. I suppose you're a younger version of him, or he would have looked like an older version of you."

He carried on looking out of the window. His hands were still now.

"Sorry," she said. "Just pretend I never said anything. Sorry, I'm so stupid sometimes."

"Maybe we looked alike," he said. "I don't know, but anyway you wouldn't see it unless you'd seen him when he was younger, I don't think. I mean he'd lost his hair, and he was finding work more and more of a strain, ever since Melanie and the job…" He looked down at the table again, then back up at her, and narrowed his eyes. Coral-blue eyes that peered at her and she could hardly stop herself from staring at them. "I'm even more surprised if Melanie didn't tell you about *that,*" he said. "If you're friends."

The silence bubbled again. Kate felt a blush threaten her skin. "Sorry," she said again. "It doesn't matter."

She looked at her own hands as her fingers rolled around each of the others.

"I can't imagine," she said finally. "Losing a parent, I mean, having a parent actually *die.* I mean, someone you're so close to like that. I can't imagine what that must be like, how you cope with that."

His face was straight and serious now. "It's surprising

how you do," he replied. "Your brain takes over and it's surprising how your body, your brain... sorts it, just keeps going and carries on."

She was watching while he spoke. He was very serious while he said the words, like he really believed it, but Kate could see that it wasn't true at all. Then he looked her full in the eyes. She could see a hint of suspicion flit in the blue of his, and a pressing for truth.

Anthony looked straight at her then. "You know he killed himself, don't you?" he said.

Kate stared at him. "Yes," she said. "I do know that."

He shook his head a little and spoke quietly, almost to himself. "Of course you do, of course you know that." He nodded now, as if she was confirming everything for him. "Well... so, he didn't die because he was ill," he said.

He looked away again and Kate felt a strange terror creep over her. She had wanted to talk about all this with... someone, someone else who knew about it already and understood, but now she wasn't sure. All of a sudden it felt too intimate, too close to real events and all the pain. He looked back at her suddenly as if he could feel how scared she was to fully talk about this.

He looked her right in the eyes again. "But you don't know any more than that, do you? You don't know *why* he killed himself."

*

One evening the week before Peter died he'd opened the front door, dog jerking at his ankles, and the cold air cling-filming his face. He looped the dog's lead over the animal's eager head and stepped outside. The gravel crunched under his feet and the dog pulled, straining its head forward while breath escaped its mouth and nose.

He'd walked the dog through the narrow streets down in Lyme. He never did this in summer. The dog would get too excited by noises and the quick movements of all the tourists. But he occasionally did it when the whole town was quiet in the off-season; he walked through the narrow streets with the dog's lead held tightly by his thigh. He envied the dog. Oblivious to the complications of life and death. Only being aware of the most basic things and never feeling the weight of worry. Not even understanding its own mortality and how fragile its life was. Peter carried that weight for both of them.

He'd got out of bed that morning and he'd looked at his wife, Susie, curled away from him, her hair messy against her upper back and shoulders like frayed and worn rope, and he'd looked down at himself, stocky in pyjamas, and he wondered what had happened. He couldn't tell if Susie was asleep anymore, or just pretending, just avoiding his eyes, his face. But he supposed his face wasn't such a pretty sight anymore. So, he couldn't blame her.

He walked the dog down past a second-hand bookshop and a low, steeply hidden café, to the end of the street where a pub stood on the opposite corner. Men who looked like mere boys to him swaggered outside the pub, pints in hand, beer making them immune from the cold and others' glances. More people seemed to be out in the open air these last couple of weeks. Celebrating, he supposed, though what there was to celebrate he had no idea. Time was careering towards Christmas, he knew that, and he could hardly face it. He stood and looked around him and he saw how much his home had changed. He didn't know who or what these people were anymore. He didn't understand young people. Felt older for thinking that. Displaced. Like his time had been and gone and now he was just waiting. But he'd never really understood young people, not since he was young himself, maybe not even then. He watched for a moment as the boys laughed, drank beer fast and hung around the doorway to the pub. He breathed the sea air slowly, sadness drifting in with salt and the thick smell of bar food.

The dog strained at his side, held tight by his fist around the lead. He turned and walked back through the little streets. Once again he envied the dog for a life with no cares: never having to spare a thought for getting kids through university, roof repairs, getting the car through its MOT, or the imminent loss of his best friend. The knowledge of the tumour swollen in the dog's chest was something Peter would never have to pass on to the dog. It would just be over soon, and the dog would die happy, spared the weeks of crippling fear.

Peter wished he could trade places.

*

In a single moment of bravery before they left the café, Kate took a pen from her bag and wrote her mobile number on a napkin. She handed it to him and watched as he hesitated, glancing at the thin paper as if it were contaminated, and then taking it cautiously and folding it into his pocket. She had no idea whether he had any intention of calling the number at all, or if he only took it out of politeness. She stared at his face. Pale skin. His hair the colour of damp sticks. Then they left together and she turned away from him outside the tearooms. He would walk back up the street now, she supposed, maybe going home, while she would round the steps again, down, and then cross the road and into the narrow street where she lived, the small, damp flat waiting.

*

She stopped as she came to the lazy corner the Pilot Boat Inn wrapped itself around. The pub she used to go to all the time with Anthony when they were together. So many evenings. What did they all amount to now?

She stood now and looked at the way Silver Street curved, hiding the top of the road from view. Behind her the sea shifted calmly. She turned to her right, where the Pilot Boat Inn bent into the narrow street beside her. She walked through the slim street until she came to the white house she used to live in. She stood and looked up at the window, a pale roller blind dropped, its heavy weighted bottom resting on the towels that lay in the sills of the windows, constantly taking the moisture from the leaking window frames. She'd been here to pick up her post about six months ago and that was the last time she'd been inside.

She stood outside the flat now, just the burst of scent

from the bakery travelling down the empty street. And she thought she'd never come back here. Once she'd done what she came here to do that would be it. Once she'd put things right. Cleared the air. Said she was sorry for all that happened. Been absolved. Like a ghost, once she'd dealt with her unfinished business, she could move on. And then she'd never come back.

*

It felt strange standing in the same spaces as Kate, but just at a different time. He thought he could feel her, the way she moved still lingering in the air, her smile still living here. He breathed the same air as she had when he walked in the factory, and he thought about the taste of her kiss and the feel of her skin.

When it was time for his break, Matthew stepped out of the back door and stood for a minute breathing the cold air. The bins to his right sat, full to their lids, and beside them another large overflow box held a jumble of rope.

He leaned over and picked a piece up.

He passed the length of rope through his hands and felt it move and slither. He grasped it for the last time in his palm, his fingers stretched around it, feeling it pull against him. Slight resistance. Slight compliance. Everything was being packed away for the day and people were wandering the building with a feeling of satisfaction and completeness. The week was done. Over. But not for Matthew. He would be back tomorrow. After an early finish today, he would come back tomorrow and get this job done before the rush of Monday morning began here again.

Matthew wandered out to the yard at the back again. Used rope was being tumbled into a skip. And he watched for a moment, leaning on the back door. Then, when the rope was settled and there was no one else there, he walked forward and leaned into the skip. He grasped the rope in his hands again and pulled it up to the surface. Heavy like it was wet. He passed the rope through his hands and over his arms until he found the right length. Then he wound it around his arm in a tight oval. He nodded to himself at the thought, then he took another piece as well and walked to the van where his hold-all waited.

*

Melanie walked up Silver Street, The Volunteer on the other side of the road, the library set back in its own plot aside from the shops, the mini-market, the Indian restaurant. She walked past all these familiar buildings and with each step she took what she was about to do seemed more and more unappealing. All of these things, this place, these people, none of it was "hers" anymore. She didn't belong here or with any of this now.

She stopped walking and looked ahead. From where she stood she could see the cars on the top road moving fast. Up there, over that road, past the bus stop and up the drive, was the house. What was she doing here? It suddenly seemed like such a stupid idea. She'd come all the way back here for this. Hadn't she? Had she really come all the way back here to do this? Standing there in the street now she felt so stupid. She was hardly going to get a great welcome up at that house. Maybe Susie would be angry, maybe she'd slam the door in Melanie's face. Or worse still, maybe Anthony would be there. The thought of that had her stuck to the spot for a moment. And then it all seemed too difficult. She couldn't imagine how she would actually go through with it. After everything that had happened.

But Susie. Susie deserved some sort of apology. At least that.

Melanie stood there. Then she made the mistake of looking around her at the street. Men, women, children, all going in and out of shops, happy about what they'd bought, living, laughing. And she couldn't do it. Facing Susie was too difficult. The thought of it now made a fear swell up in her middle. She didn't have to do it. They didn't know she was here. She didn't have to do anything she didn't want to.

*

Clean bed sheets folded and piled, freshly ironed, on the edge of the bed. Kate smoothed them with her hand as she moved past them. The door opened in the next room and Matthew came into the flat. He sometimes finished early on Friday afternoons, if he could manage it, and she heard him moving in the kitchen now, probably unbuttoning his overalls already and lowering them to remove them from his body.

"Hey!" she called. "You want a drink or anything?"

She could hear him take off his heavy boots and drop them by the back door.

"I need to have a shower," he said. "Won't be a minute."

She followed the sound of him through the flat, but when she reached the bathroom he'd already run the water and had stepped into the cubicle. The heat from the shower filled the space outside the bathroom door as she closed it slightly again and went to the kitchen. She tutted to herself as she picked up the overalls from the table and went to put them in the wash. She stopped and looked back at the table, the neck of Matthew's overalls tight in her hand. As she moved them, they revealed two lengths of rope curled on the table like lazy letter Os.

There was a knock on the door, and when Kate opened it, she looked into the woman's face, trying to figure the shape of the eyes and the way the mouth curled into an almost-there smile, almost not.

"Hi," the woman said. "Sorry to bother you, I just thought, while I was back in Lyme I'd call down and see if you'd got any post here for me, you know, any that maybe you hadn't got the chance to send on... I mean, I know, I understand you probably don't have time to do that, so I thought... while I was here... to be honest I wasn't expecting anyone to be in, with it being Friday afternoon. I thought you'd both be at work."

"Oh, God... oh, you're..."

"Melanie. I used to live here...? Before."

Before. Before the notes in the Christmas cards started to come. Before Peter died. Before. Kate stared at her. She was Melanie. This was Melanie. The same Melanie. It ran in her brain and she tried to sort it quickly. She recognised her. Somehow. From somewhere. But Kate had never met Melanie before... had she? There was something about the shape of her face.

Kate looked behind her, back into the flat. The steam from the shower was floating into the kitchen and she could hear Matthew singing to himself as he stepped from the bathroom into the bedroom.

"Sorry," she said. "Now's not a good time, but if you can come back, I'll look out any post for you that we've kept."

She saw Melanie's eyes flit behind her into the flat. She gave a little smile. "Feels weird," she said. "Being back here and seeing someone else living here."

"Sorry," Kate said. "How about you come back tomorrow? It's just..." She jerked her thumb behind her to show that she had things going on right now.

"Of course, yes, sorry, I didn't mean to intrude. Yes, maybe I'll be able to pop by tomorrow."

Kate closed the door and turned back into the flat, instantly regretting asking Melanie to come back. She should have just found the post and handed it over. Got rid of her. The whole thing was awkward to say the least. She looked up. Matthew was standing in the doorway of the kitchen, the damp air from the shower behind him, his hair wet, jeans just pulled on.

"I see you found" – he motioned to the table – "what I brought home," he said.

Kate walked to the table and touched one of the coils of rope. "Yeah," she said. "What's this all about then?"

He shrugged, then watched her finger gently brush the rope before pulling away. "I thought you might like it," he said.

She looked up at him and frowned. "What do you mean?"

"Well, I thought maybe we could... have some fun."

*

The day he came back from taking the dog out, he felt the drag in his feet as he walked the path towards his house. He looked down at the dog, panting from running through the undercliff, and he felt his whole body heavy on him. Like a coat. Like worry. He stopped on the path, just before the overhanging tress opened up to reveal the big house and the garden, the gravel drive and the cars, and he stood. He looked down at the dog again, sitting now obediently by his side, waiting and wondering why. He bent a little and slipped the lead free of the dog. Then he stood there and waited, the lead hanging from his hand, the dog still looking up and waiting.

*

Kate felt a blush race through her veins and rise quickly into her skin.

"You mean...?"

He shrugged again. "Why not?" he said. "You might like it. You know you can trust me, I wouldn't hurt you, and if you don't..."

She put her hand up to signal a stop. "Wait, wait." she said. "Of course I trust you, but..."

"Kate, we haven't... and I just thought, you know, it's been a little while and we haven't... and I know you've been... stressed, but... I just thought, maybe this... I mean, it's been *ages* and maybe we, maybe you..." He motioned to the rope again, curled on the table between them. "It's just role-play."

She shook her head slowly. "Why would you think that?" she asked. "I mean, why would you think I would want... I just don't understand you, Matthew. How could you?"

"You don't understand me?" he shouted. "I'm easy to understand, Kate, it's really not that complicated. I have needs, you know! I just thought something *different* might get you back in the mood. You're the one who's hard to understand, you're the confusing one!"

*

That was weird. Seeing that girl, Kate today. Bumping into her like that and the way she just went for a drink with him as if it was completely normal. As if they knew each other. The whole thing was weird.

Anthony sat in his room at home in the dark. His mum was downstairs, watching Friday night TV, but Anthony hardly ever sat with her now. It was too uncomfortable. They couldn't talk about dad, but it was always there in the room with them. They couldn't not talk about it. So they didn't talk about anything and Anthony would rather sit on his own than feel that tension all the time.

Kate had seemed to understand, which was also weird. They didn't know each other and yet Anthony had felt he could talk to her.

He held the paper she'd written her phone number on and looked at the way the numbers curled. It wasn't like she was flirting with him. He was sure he'd recognise it if she had been. It was something else. Like she really did just want to talk. The only thing he couldn't work out was, why?

*

The house Melanie was staying in while she was here was fitted with blinds in every room. Slatted wooden blinds that, no matter how you tried to close them tight, always held gaps between their slightly sun-warped slices of varnished wood.

Melanie had drifted off to sleep with the stars quivering in the dark sky, shining like specks of light on water through the gaps in the blinds. She'd woken as if she was coming up for air and almost sat up in bed.

It was a stupid dream. She lay back down in the bed and felt her breathing return to normal. When she woke up again she could hear her own heart thumping in her body, blood pulsing, a throbbing beat in her ears. It took her a minute to fit together what was going on. The same dream again. She was knocking on the door at the house in Uplyme.

The third time, she'd woken as if she was scared of being asleep. Susie had answered the door, but had a strange expression on her face. She wasn't angry or pleased, she looked...

unhappy, and more than that, she looked upset and timid, and maybe even a little frightened. Then Melanie had peered into the house behind Susie and there, moving slightly like a shadow, like a blurred image on film, was Peter.

This wasn't going to go away. She turned over in the bed, away from the bright moon. This wasn't going to leave her alone until she'd done what she came here to do.

*

The moon was so bright through the bedroom window it woke her like the flicker of a lighthouse. She blinked and stared up at it, poking through the gap in the curtains. As a child, she'd always thought a bright, round, clear moon was a sign of something. She'd have believed this moment, her waking to it shining right at her like this, would have meant something. Was an omen of some sort. A portent. But now she knew it was just the moon.

She turned slightly in the bed. Matthew was asleep beside her, turned away from her. He'd stayed up watching TV while she came to bed, slipped quietly in beneath the cold sheets and then pretended to be asleep when he finally did join her. Like she did every night. Every night since it happened.

She moved her face away from Matthew again, and looked over at the low chest of drawers below the window. There the rope lay, an S shape under the moonlight, where she had thrown it when she'd tidied the kitchen table for tea, where she'd left it, one glance back at it as she walked away and back into the kitchen, its scratchy body, its frayed skin, staring back at her.

He didn't speak the next morning, made no reference to the argument or the rope lying still curled around on the chest of drawers in the bedroom. Kate knew that was his way. That was how he dealt with things. He left the flat and the uncomfortable silence and went to work.

Kate took a damp cloth and began her daily ritual of wiping skirting boards and cupboard tops, watching the clock and hoping that Melanie wasn't planning to come early. She finished and then struggled with the hoover in the tiny cupboard, bringing it out awkwardly like stifled truths, forced lies. She vacuumed every corner of the flat then stood back and looked at the clean lines of walls meeting skirting boards, meeting plain cream carpet, dust-free surfaces and tidy shelves. This was how she had to keep it all the time. Drove Matthew mad. This was the only way she could have it. Couldn't stand it when he made a mess and didn't clear up. Couldn't bear to see dust collect on the TV or drinks spilled not wiped up, even teacups left on the side in the kitchen and not washed. Couldn't take it if the place was a mess. And anyway, it was best to keep busy, especially today, in case Melanie arrived.

*

Melanie looked around when she came into the flat, noting changes and the alien presence of someone else's things where hers had once been.

"Come in, sit down," Kate said, walking quickly ahead of Melanie and motioning to the living room, to the sofa. "Can I get you a tea or coffee or anything?"

"Tea, yes, thanks."

Melanie could hear Kate moving round in the kitchen, putting the kettle on and taking mugs from a cupboard. It was strange how she still felt some ownership of those things. A different kettle. Different mugs. But still, where she herself had once moved and made tea and cooked and lived.

Then Kate reappeared, leaving the whir of the kettle building up momentum in the background. "Well, I'm not sure that we've got that much for you, you know, I don't think that much has come here." She turned to the mantelpiece where the old fireplace had once been, now bricked up and hidden, fronted by a modern coffee table. "Just these," she said, and she took a small pile of what looked like junk mail, sat down on the sofa and handed them to Melanie.

Melanie took the post and then looked around the room. "It's weird being back here," she said. "And I don't just mean the flat, I mean it's weird being back here altogether, being back in Lyme."

Kate paused for a moment and looked at Melanie. She was plain. Nothing special.

"So, you don't live there anymore," Kate said. "At the address you gave me?"

"Oh, I never did really, well, just for a few months… but I knew I wasn't staying there, it's just an address, friends who forward mail onto me and stuff. I moved in with them for a while before… before I left. I'd been planning on getting my own place, buying I mean, not renting anymore, it's dead money, isn't it, renting? But, well, anyway, it didn't turn out that way in the end. It was convenient at the time though, especially for work; bus stop's right outside the house and drops off just down the street from the rope factory."

Kate felt a fear burn in her chest. The rope factory. Did Melanie just say she worked at the rope factory? The words from Peter's niece at the funeral came back to her then: *... and you worked with her of course, you're from the same company.* She stared at her, trying desperately to place her from the factory.

"I'm staying with them now while I'm back," Melanie was saying.

Kate hesitated. Her mind was racing. "So, where is it you live now then?" she said.

"Portugal," Melanie said.

"Portugal?" Kate asked. She could feel the hot blush on her neck and cheeks. "Why Portugal? I mean, how come? How come you live there?"

Melanie wafted her hand to show how unimportant this was. "Oh, I didn't pick the place, well, it was either that or staying in Lyme for the rest of my life and, I mean, come on, not a huge decision to make, is it?" she laughed now, and Kate stared hard at her face. She did remember her. She looked a lot different now. The make-up was gone. The brightly dyed hair gone. The clothes toned down and more sombre, more melancholy. But she did recognise her. Melanie should recognise her too. Surely. Though now she thought about it, Kate was always too junior to have been on Melanie's radar. They hadn't exactly mingled in the same circles at the rope factory. Technically, Melanie was the head of Kate's department but they had never even spoken to each other, and Melanie seemed to be the kind of person who never had much to do with those beneath her.

However, Melanie peered back at her then, as if Kate had actually spoken it; as if she could hear Kate's thoughts or it was so plain on her face, so transparent.

"I'm sorry," Melanie said. And she looked at her like she was seeing her for the first time. "But, do I know you?"

Kate made an over-emphasised expression of confusion.

"I mean, from somewhere else," Melanie went on. "I mean not from this flat and all that, but..."

They looked at each other for a moment and Kate felt the facts slipping. It was only a moment, and then it was gone.

Melanie shook her head. "Sorry," she said. "Doesn't matter."

"Anyway let me get on with our cuppas," said Kate. "Do you take milk and sugar?"

*

Peter followed his grandfather. Followed the rope. As if he was holding the other end, thick and heavy like a tug-of-war rope, wrapped over his body like he was the anchor man. And his grandfather leading him, pulling, turning back and smiling slightly at Peter as a boy. *You can trust the rope, not like people.* The rope made them a living, always had. It would carry on making them a living. Peter followed the family line, felt his way along, his hands grasping at the steady, sturdy rope. He wouldn't live it like his grandfather had, those days were gone. He wouldn't turn it in his hands and pull it tight and work it into different lengths, different thicknesses, different uses. He wouldn't display his palms to his eyes and rub his fingers over the blisters that formed there. But he would be as close as he could to all that. Modern rope manufacturing. He said it proudly. Pleased with the way this industry had evolved and become what it now was. Happy that it stayed in this quiet part of southern

England. It was his business. His family's legacy. He went to the rope factory straight from school. Couldn't imagine any other area of work he would want. Couldn't see any other life.

*

It was in the flat. How could she have forgotten? How could she have let slide the fact that it was there and now she was there.

Kate brought their cups of tea into the living room where Melanie was waiting. She stopped in the doorway, holding the mugs, looking first at the mugs in her hand to monitor the risk of spilling, then up at Melanie, standing by the TV, her hand up at the wall, her fingers tucked under the edge of the Christmas card.

"Oh I see you know Susie and Anthony," she said.

Kate stared at her. "Er… yes, sort of."

"Sort of?" Melanie said, force heavy in her words. "You've got a card here that Susie has written. So how do you know them?"

"Well, I don't really… I mean..."

"So why do you have a Christmas card from Susie and Anthony on your wall?"

She could have lied. Could have said she opened it by mistake and then decided to put it up anyway. She probably should have lied. Of all the times she lied this was probably the time when she should have. But she didn't. She walked into the room and carefully put the mugs down on a side table. She could feel the blush hot on her skin. Lying probably wasn't an option now anyway. Her pause and her motion and her honest skin had more than likely already sealed it.

"I opened it," she blurted out.

Melanie narrowed her eyes. "What do you mean? You mean it wasn't for you?"

Kate shook her head.

"It was to me? This was meant for me?"

"Yes," Kate said. "And I opened it, so..."

"So, why put it on your wall?"

Kate let out the tense breath she'd been keeping in. "That's a good question," she said.

"Well?"

"Well, I... I suppose it wasn't like any other card I'd had. It was more... personal."

Melanie was frowning. "Personal?"

"It… it had a note with it."

"A note?"

"Yes. For you."

"What note?"

"It was to tell you about Peter, about the funeral."

Melanie was staring at Kate, a frown edging in between her eyebrows. Her skin prickled at the mention of Peter.

"It just said that really, that he'd died, when the funeral was and that they were doing fine."

"Doing fine?" Melanie asked.

"Yes."

"Did it mention Anthony? Was it from him?"

"No. No, it was from Susie."

She searched Melanie's face for any sign the mood was lifted. Found none.

She went on. "He's OK… Anthony... if you…" she stopped herself. Melanie was looking at her hard.

"I can't believe this," she said. "Why didn't you tell me?"

"I... sorry... I didn't think it was my place."

"That letter, that card, they were for me. To tell me I was welcome at the funeral! The card was addressed to me, so why didn't you even forward it on, once you realised it was important? I think it was very much your place to tell me, since you'd opened it!"

Melanie's face was creeping with a flush of anger. She looked away from Kate for a moment and out of the old familiar window. Standing in this flat again was giving her the weird sensation of being suffocated. There was lots more she could say but she needed to get out. Out of this room, this flat, this small town.

Melanie eyed the mugs of tea on the table. She didn't want to stay here a minute more than she had to.

"Right," she said. "I'd better go and see her, sort this thing out once and for all."

*

The rope factory was out of town. Away from the trendy bars and cafes with circular metal tables and wobbly chairs outside on the pavements. Away from the bookshops and small boutiques, where tourists browsed in summer and trade slowed in winter. Out of the town centre, beating with the steady rhythm of its year-round shift patterns, set apart from the routines of Bridport life.

Matthew had followed the roads to the rope factory where he would work again today, redecorating the offices. He'd thought again about Kate and how it might be for her when she was at work. The conversations over coffee at break time, the boredom of office life, the smiles across the room and the hope for something exciting to leap into the day. He realised he knew almost nothing about what Kate did here. Even less about the people she worked with and how they got on. She hardly ever talked about it, and even less now, even less since…

He got out of the van in the car park and looked at the building she inhabited for so much of her waking hours. Strange that she should have this other life here that he knew so little about. Strange that it should be so separate to everything else they did together.

He felt the familiar twist of jealousy. She had a whole other life here. A side of her life he didn't see. She spent time with people he didn't know and had conversations he never heard. He didn't know what she did or how she acted here. He wasn't to know if she flirted with every man she came across.

He stood in the car park and looked at all the windows, people passing, going up and down flights of stairs and talking on phones. He wondered if he should pick her up from the factory himself when she went back to work: he wondered if that would make it easier for her to go back. It would also mean he could keep an eye on her. Maybe he could have a word with his partner and swing it so he could be let off to in time to drive her home every day.

Matthew was thinking through how that might work. He could imagine selling the idea to Kate easily enough, making a big thing of how considerate he was being. But he was pretty sure he wouldn't be able to do mornings as well and bring her in. That meant she'd still be getting the bus and walking from the bus stop and spending time between the bus dropping her off and her start time at work. And who knew what might be going on in that time? You couldn't trust women. You couldn't trust anyone for that matter. People were unreliable. Matthew knew that.

*

Melanie left the flat, the tea going cold in the mug on the table. She walked through the alleyway, just as she had hundreds of times when she'd lived here. She walked through the narrow streets and then up onto Silver Street. Up past the pub and the small supermarket, the library on the other side of the road, The Volunteer, up to the top of the street where the main road ran. She crossed the road and came to the bottom of the long driveway.

Melanie didn't stop or really think about what she was doing until she was standing at the door, knocking, and she could see Susie coming from the kitchen to open it.

The look of surprise on Susie's face gave Melanie's chest a jolt.

"Hi," she said. "Can I come in?"

For a moment the two women stared at each other, neither of them knowing what would happen next.

"Melanie," Susie said. "I didn't think you were around."

"No, I wasn't, but... I came back to... can I come in?"

Susie held the door open wider and Melanie walked

inside. She'd been in this house countless times, but it felt different now. The absence of Peter and the way he'd left had caused a shift in the house's emotions. It felt quieter and emptier, but also more peaceful.

"You didn't come to the funeral," Susie was saying as she walked through to the kitchen. "I mean, I understand and everything, though you would have been quite welcome, you know."

Melanie could feel herself become almost shy in front of this woman whose husband had died so recently. This woman she'd known and spent time with, but now seemed like a stranger.

"I didn't think... I mean, Anthony, he wouldn't have wanted me there. To be honest, I didn't think you would have wanted me there."

Susie was filling the kettle at the sink. She turned around and put it down on the worktop. "You look different," she said. "I like your hair."

Melanie touched the bottom of her hairline, running her fingers through the new short length.

"Anthony doesn't know what he wants most of the time," Susie went on. "But he didn't want you to leave like you did, that's for sure."

Melanie held onto her hair for a second then let go and let her hand fall to her side. "I know," she said. "I won't stay. I mean, I can't, it's just..."

"So why are you here then? He's not here at the moment but you will see him, won't you?"

"I don't know. I don't know if it's a good idea or not. I had thought I would, but now..."

"So why come at all?"

"I wanted to say I'm sorry. To you. For all the trouble I caused. For all that happened, all the... mess. I wanted to say, I'm sorry for everything."

*

Anthony called the same afternoon. A phone call straight from the edge of all that seemed likely. The day had stretched out and rumbled on and Kate was thinking there was no way, he wouldn't be in contact. But then he called. As if time meant nothing. She imagined him unfolding the paper napkin she'd written her number on and reading it and thinking about her, her face and the things she'd said bleeding through with the numbers on the napkin.

Kate could almost feel Anthony's voice stumbling in the phone line. "Hi, it's… it's Anthony… from, erm… yesterday."

She saved him. "Anthony, yes, hi."

"I was just thinking… about what you'd said, about that stuff… My dad, and… you know Melanie and… maybe we could meet again…"

Kate could feel his need stretching through to her. A need to know more, to gather information, anecdotes, sights and sounds of a past he couldn't touch anymore. She felt it melt into her and wondered if he realised she needed the same things.

"Yeah great," she said.

"Well, if you're not busy this afternoon…"

"Ok, that's fine. I'm not busy. Shall we go to the tearooms again?"

She thought about Anthony's days, never being busy, always being a drag.

"Yeah, sure," he said.

In the tearooms later that same day, she looked at him. Of course he was good-looking. But she gazed into his face and felt the disappointment pool and collect inside her. It wasn't enough. Somehow she was hoping that just being with him would help her with the grieving process. But he wasn't enough to cover it all over.

"So, you said you were thinking about what I'd said, about your dad..."

He looked down at his fingers on the table. Clean fingernails. Soft, pale hands. "Oh yeah," he said. "I was thinking, you know, when you asked about him, and me... no one has really asked me about him. They ask my brothers, and Mum of course, well, they ask how she is, not really about him."

"Well, of course," she said. "No one wants to ask about the person who is gone because they think it will upset you. So they ask if you're OK, that kind of thing, but, it's like no one wants to talk about the person who is gone."

He looked up, straight in her eyes. She felt the water blue of them shoot into her. "Exactly," he said. "And the thing is, there are things..."

He wouldn't tell her yet. Anthony felt his shame wriggle under his skin, trying to break free, reminding him that he knew he would feel so much better once he'd told, spoken about this thing that dragged him further towards the ground every day. But he wouldn't tell her yet.

She was waiting for him to continue speaking. "It doesn't matter," he said.

"Well, it kinda does," she said. "Why did you say it was your fault? Your dad...?"

He looked around him at the other people in the tearooms. He thought about lowering his voice to carry on with this mis-shaped conversation, but he needed to get out. He couldn't speak about this and risk his words, free in this room, travelling the air like the common cold or tiny flies.

"Do you mind if we go?" he asked.

"Go?"

"Yeah, do you mind if we go outside, go for a walk, I just don't want to talk about this... *here.*"

They stood up to leave and even the scrape of the chairs on the tiled floor seemed too loud to Anthony, too conspicuous. Once they were out in the cold air everything seemed easier.

He took a deep breath, deeper, he thought, than he'd gone in ages. "I don't mean *actually.* You know, obviously, I didn't... kill him or anything, but I mean... I'm to blame."

She looked up at him in the darkness. Forceful. "You're not," she said.

He stayed silent. She knew nothing about it. Of course she would say that. Anyone would. But she didn't know anything about it.

They carried on silently for a moment, until he felt her draw her own breath deep, words ready to be free.

"What did you mean when you said Peter, your dad I mean, suffered for years? What did he suffer with?"

Anthony kept his head down. "Is this what you wanted to talk about?" he asked.

"I'm just trying to understand."

"Why? Why does it matter to you?"

"It just does, please, Anthony, I need to know."

He stopped walking and looked at her, trying to work it out. "Look," he said. "I don't want you to think I'm some sort of psycho or anything. When I said he suffered and that it was my fault, I didn't mean literally, I didn't mean..."

"Of course, I didn't think that. I didn't think you'd killed him, silly!"

He nodded. "He was under a lot of pressure, that's all."

She frowned. "What pressure?"

"At work. It really got to him sometimes and he couldn't sleep properly. He suffered with stress for years because of his job. But, at home as well…" He stopped and she felt the end of his words.

"I didn't know," she said, then she turned quickly to look at Anthony. "Do you think that's why…?"

For a moment everything was peeled and they spoke to each other as if they both knew the truth.

Anthony shrugged. "We'll never know," he said. But his own certainty moved again inside him, pulsed in his muscles. He knew.

They walked down to the beach and sat on the pebbles, watching as the sea constantly moved, never stopping, stretching out under the dark sky till it was just a shimmer with the night. Anthony could feel some of the things he kept in begin to bubble under his skin. Had no idea why he would tell this girl these things.

"But you said it was your fault," Kate said. "What did

you mean? Why would you say that?"

"I've done some stupid things in my time," Anthony said. "And the thing is, you don't realise until it's too late how much those things affect your parents."

She waited, still looking into his eyes. She could see the words dissolve back into him. He shook his head. "Doesn't matter," he said again.

She stopped walking, forcing him to stop too and look at her. "Well, like I said before," she said. "It kinda does. Sometimes you need to talk about that person, I think, it's just that others are uncomfortable with it if you do... but I'm not, I wouldn't be uncomfortable, I understand."

He was looking at her, trying to decide if he should trust her. He was wondering if she'd lost someone too. Wondering if she'd really understand. Doubting it. He looked ahead of him again. The bay dark down there. Lights from the hotel and restaurant to the right. It was gone. What was he thinking? He couldn't tell a virtual stranger these things. He kept looking down to the bay and a silence settled. Kate followed his gaze out to the sea. She stood closer to his side and forced a change into the air between them.

"I meant to tell you, something a bit… well, unexpected, happened earlier," she said.

Anthony turned back to face her. His bearded chin low so it almost touched his chest.

"What's that?" he asked.

She thought about Melanie sitting in the flat with her, handling the post and gazing around the room, at the Christmas tree, the cards on the silver rope on the wall, the card meant for her with the skaters on the front and the note inside it about Peter. Melanie whose name made Anthony struggle and blush whenever it was spoken to him.

"I saw Melanie."

He looked at her quickly. Kate saw a small swallow travel down his neck.

"Was that unexpected?" he asked.

Kate ignored the question. "She looks really different,"

she went on. "Changed."

"What do you mean?"

"Just... doesn't look like the same person. Her hair is really short and her clothes... you wouldn't recognise her."

He made a look of surprise at her. "Of course I'd recognise her," he said.

She'd gone too far. She'd put her intimacy with this man above Melanie's. When, really, Kate wasn't intimate with *this* man at all. She felt the circling inside her of all the things she knew. Felt them grow. Felt them taking up too much space.

"You know she's living in Portugal now," she said.

He looked into her face for any hint that she was lying. She had to be lying.

"What?" he said. "What do you mean?"

"When she moved, she moved to Portugal. She's back here visiting."

"Why didn't you tell me that before?" he asked. "When I asked you if she was still in Dorset. You must have known, why didn't you say?"

"Should I have?"

The truth of them not knowing the other's head buzzed. Anthony's face crept with blood. He turned quickly without a word and walked away from her.

*

Anthony walked back up the street and stood outside the church. He looked at its pale walls, its dark roof, its angular shape, its head high up in the white sky. Up there, in the tower, bells like the domes of basilicas stood still and waited to be filled with sound. Below them the rope hung limp, in the hands of bell ringers on a Sunday and one night a week, pulled taut, tight till there was nowhere else for it to go, then unravelling, sound so loud it would deafen. Sound that dropped inside everyone who heard it and vibrated through them. No way anyone could stand beneath them, he thought. No way anyone could take it.

He'd done what he always does. He'd felt the discomfort swaddling his body and he'd got up and run, turned away, got out of there as quickly as he could. It wasn't her fault. Sometimes he just couldn't face these things when they came towards him like that. If he could tell someone he would have done it already. It weighed his flesh down, all this. Keeping it inside. It made him feel sick and light-headed to think about it. It moved inside of him over and over and there was no way to push it out of his body. There should have been someone he could tell. Not his mother obviously. Not his brothers.

He thought about telling Kate, that girl. That insistent girl who had appeared in his life, from where or how he didn't know. But she was there. Maybe he could tell her. He thought about how the words would sound if they were released from his head. He wondered what she'd think, how she'd take it. It shouldn't matter to her. It wouldn't be personal to her.

*

For as long as Anthony could remember it had been in their lives. All of them, in one way or another. Of course his older brothers got away with it because they had good jobs, following good educations. But not Anthony. For some reason Anthony's dad had taken his hopes of some strange line in occupation and had attached them to him. Anthony was the youngest. He wondered if that had anything to do with it. His brothers had done well at school, gone to university, and chosen good careers. Who could argue with that? What kind of parent wouldn't be happy with that? But not Anthony. Anthony was the last one. When the time was coming up for him to leave school he realised he was the last hope. He didn't even know why his father saw it as a hope. Anthony didn't see much hope in it.

"It's a good job," his dad had said to him. "Think about it. That's all I ask."

But, of course, that wasn't all he asked.

"You know my grandfather was a rope maker. Not like today, of course, not like it is now. He was an actual rope maker, before the factory was even built."

"Yeah, you've told me."

"So, you understand what this means to me."

"Not really, no," Anthony said. "It's not even as if it's a company that started in the family or anything. It's just a job. It's hardly the same as what your granddad did, is it?"

"Maybe not. Maybe. But it's a job for life, Anthony, these days..."

And on he went. Anthony still didn't have a full-time job. Like his brothers did. So it was the same lecture again and again every time a job was going to come up at the factory. A job for life! Anthony couldn't think of a worse fate. He had no intention of taking a job there.

But he knew someone who would. Anthony knew someone who really wanted a new job, a better job, someone who would jump at the chance of that job and make the most of it and had the skills and experience to be good at it. And she did, she was.

He told his dad. Melanie's looking for a job, she could do it. His dad had eyed him in an almost suspicious way and said nothing. So Anthony told her to go for it. And she got the job. He knew she would. Melanie was like that. Not only that, but she had also got herself a promotion soon after getting her foot in the door.

Anthony had thought for the briefest moment that this could make his dad happy. But it didn't. She was the wrong person. Anthony beamed at his dad and said wasn't it great. But Peter looked at him in the same way he always looked at him. Disappointment sleeping under his skin and waking slowly. Bemusement. And this time something else too. This time something that wasn't connected to Anthony, was just about Peter and her, and yet somehow made Anthony feel at fault.

*

He needed to breathe. He stood by the church. Leaned against it and felt the walls rough against his skin. He'd meet her later and then maybe he'd tell her. Maybe he would feel better after. He thought about the moments that would follow on. What her face would look like. What she would say to him. How things would be after. He thought maybe he would be alone again then. The thought made a place under his ribs fall deep into his belly.

He took his phone from his pocket and sent her a short text. 'Meet me 2nite. In the pub up the road, the Volunteer, about 8.' Then he felt for his breath, shaking in his lungs, tried to calm it by taking it in deeper, and he turned and walked home.

*

Kate had a lie ready. It wasn't difficult. She'd used it once or twice before and it was so likely anyway that she never felt bad about saying it, never really felt as if it was a lie.

"Matt, I've got to go over to my mum's. Claire's left the kids again and Mum has to go out." She knew Matthew would never offer to go with her, not if it was for babysitting. He found kids a scary prospect, a confusion. And unnecessary in his life. Plus he was always happy to have some time alone in the flat. Kate could almost hear him switching on the Playstation already.

"OK," he said. "I'll see you later then."

She couldn't dress up or Matthew would find that strange, not that she had much to dress up in. She kept her jeans on and changed her top. Kept her jacket wrapped around her chest so Matt didn't notice. Looked at him as she left the flat, sitting on the floor, bare feet stretched out on the carpet, dark-blue jeans, hair like a grass-topped sand dune, Playstation ready.

The kink of rope still sat on the chest of drawers where she'd left it. They hadn't spoken about it. But Kate could feel the questions bubbling like oil behind Matthew's eyes when he looked at her.

She left the flat, went slowly down the narrow stairs, up the alley between the buildings and out onto the slim street. She looked up at their window. She wasn't cheating. Not really. There was no reason to feel guilty. She was searching for a connection, that's all. Fumbling for some link, some physical, solid form that would keep her brain in touch with what was lost. Anthony was it. He was a living, breathing connection.

*

When Anthony was twelve the words shuddered in the air at his new secondary school. They were directed like cruise missiles at his ears, and became so frequent, so weighty, he could feel them stacked up inside him until he couldn't stand it any longer. He wondered if his brothers might have stood up for him if they had been there, if they hadn't both been away at university by then.

Something had to give. Something had to spill. He had lowered his face every time he'd heard the shouts in the corridors, *Oi nerd*, and the whispered and hissed words in the yard, *Mummy's boy*, until his skin couldn't burn anymore and his eyes couldn't continue turning away. There was no way to live like this.

Anthony's mum was away at her sister's for a couple of days, so he decided it was a good time to approach his dad about it.

"There's this boy," he said.

His dad looked up from gathering the autumn leaves strewn across the lawn.

"He's been calling me names and pushing me around."

"What names?"

Anthony mumbled, the embarrassment prickling in his throat. "Nerd, stuff like that."

Peter took a breath in slowly through his nose and stood up straight. He'd never had to deal with anything like this with his other two sons. Trouble never seemed to touch them at all. But Anthony was different. He was the youngest and all the possible problems that could have hit his two older brothers, but missed, appeared to be landing on Anthony. Peter could feel a small prickle of anger inside himself. It shifted and he wasn't sure if it was because of the boy doing the bullying or Anthony for allowing it to happen. "Who is this boy?" he asked. "What's his name?"

Anthony thought about concealing the name, telling his dad he couldn't say it, the boy would kill him, but he saw by the look on his dad's face that there was no way he could escape this.

"Stuart Mace," he said.

The sound of the boy's name fell inside Peter. It collected his anger and then ran with it through his body. "There's only one way to deal with bullies, Anthony," Peter said. "What you need to do is you need to walk right up to this Stuart and, in front of all his friends, punch him right in the face. Show him and everyone else that you won't be pushed around. You stand up to him, that's what you do."

He patted Anthony on the shoulder as he walked past him and back into the house.

At school the next day the air seemed sharper, every moment that passed in class seemed to have an edge that fizzed, more than a normal Friday. He waited for it to happen. He could feel them gather together when they left the classroom, bundling for comfort and security, shunting down the corridor behind him. They uttered a few words and laughed, but Anthony kept walking, his eyes on the polished lino on the floor. He reached the door where the sun broke the suffocation of school. As he leaned on the door Stuart shoved him from behind and he stumbled through, his weighty, heavy body swaying and grappling with confusion. He stood upright and turned to face Stuart. He was laughing and looking right at Anthony, his friends straggly behind him like torn wallpaper still hanging from a wall. Anthony thought about it for half a second then he punched Stuart in the face. Everything seemed to go in slow motion, until his fist hit. It felt good. Anthony might have even been grinning. But Stuart's face filled up with uncontrollable emotion and madness and he laid into Anthony like he had never done. In front of all his friends.

When he got home Anthony tried to hide away in his room, but his dad came up to see him as soon as he got in from work. Like he expected it. Like he knew it would end in disaster for Anthony.

"What happened to your mouth?" Peter asked.

"I did as you said," he answered. "I hit him."

"And?"

"And he hit me back, even harder. Everyone was there. They all saw. Now they all think I'm stupid. Thanks a lot."

For just a second Peter felt out of his depth. This had never happened with his other two sons. He didn't understand this one. He didn't seem to be like the other two, or like Peter at all.

Then he told him it was the right thing to do anyway. "You've got to stand up to bullies," he said.

Anthony waited until later to look at all his bruises in the mirror. Stuart had been clever – he had mostly avoided Anthony's face, apart from the split lip which had spilt some blood onto his clothes. But Anthony didn't need a mirror to know that he was bruised all over.

On the Sunday night Susie came home. She pulled her small case through the front door and began chatting about her sister and her niece and everything they'd said and done before she'd even taken her coat off. Peter took her case and said he'd put the kettle on and didn't say a word about anything else. Maybe she wouldn't notice. Maybe there'd be no need to bring it up at all. Somewhere, deep in every muscle of his body, Peter knew how unlikely that was.

The cuts and bruising around Anthony's lip had gone down a lot, but inevitably she noticed them as soon as Anthony came down for dinner.

Peter instantly saw in her eyes that she wouldn't leave it alone until she got to the bottom of it. She was like that, Peter thought. No use trying to back out of it. No use covering up. She'd have you in a corner before you knew what was going on.

"It's nothing," he told her. "Just this kid at school who got a bit… over-excited."

"Over-excited?" she demanded.

Peter didn't look at Anthony. He hadn't planned to make up a story on his son's behalf but somehow he felt as if he needed to be on the defensive.

"Well, it was just a bit of horseplay…" he started. He wished now he'd had the sense to collude with Anthony in advance about getting the story straight. "That's right, Anthony, isn't it…?"

Anthony was just staring at him; he didn't know what to say.

"And boys will be boys, you know, and all that," Peter was stuttering, "… and well, Anthony got thrown against a door and cut his lip – but it was all accidentally!"

"Accidentally on purpose?" she scowled, turning towards Anthony.

Anthony tried to find his voice. "No Mum, it was just an accident..."

But they could both tell she didn't believe him. She was staring at Peter and he realised he was the one back in the firing line. "So what do you propose we should do about it?" Susie demanded.

Peter shrugged.

"We've got to report it," she said. "He can't get away with this."

Peter moved his hand in the air above the table as if pushing down. "Hang on a minute, let's not over-react."

"Over-react? His lip has been cut. But it could have been worse… he might have lost a tooth! Or an eye!"

Anthony could feel the situation getting out of control. Stuart Mace would kill him if the school got involved. Stuart wouldn't care if he was expelled. He didn't care about school, but he'd kill Anthony for telling.

"No, Mum, please!" he said. "Just leave it please. It's fine now anyway."

"Fine?"

"Yeah, it was nothing. Me and Stuart are good friends and he was just messing about."

Peter caught his son's eye. He knew. Anthony knew that Peter didn't want to lose face here either. He knew his dad wouldn't want to have to admit any responsibility for what had happened.

"You see, Susie," he said. "It's fine, all worked out, no need to go getting the school involved."

Susie hesitated. She looked from her husband to her son then back again. She still felt excluded. Like there was a whole world of stuff going on here she wasn't part of. But Anthony looked mortified at the idea of her contacting school about this. It would embarrass him. She could see that.

"Well, if you're sure," she said. "This time. But if it happens again, I'll be straight down that school..."

"OK, Mum," Anthony said. "OK."

*

There was a real fire burning in The Volunteer. The pub was small and looked like it might once have been someone's living room. The bar curled round like a bend in nylon rope, discarded and left to go its own way.

Anthony was sitting in the window seat. His long hair was tucked behind his ears and he played with his moustache and beard, stroking the hair with his fingertips as if it was a dog's head. He edged his way out of the seat and went up to the bar to buy Kate a drink. She wanted to ask him where he'd been today, what he'd been doing and why the mention of Melanie had made him bolt like that earlier.

He came back to the table with a cold glass of white wine, steadied the stem as he put it down. Kate looked at his fingers. His skin was smooth and slightly pink. The whites of his knuckles showed as his hand bent, like the bones were struggling to break free. She thought about the hands of an older man, of Peter maybe, and tried to compare. Those older hands were softer, warmer, browned by days in the sun. They were relaxed and not uptight like Anthony's hands.

He sat down beside her and stared at the table. She moved a little closer.

"Are you OK?" she asked.

He leaned forward and clasped his hands around his pint glass. Kate could just see the froth of his pint about his fingers, encased, settling inside the glass.

"Yeah," he said. "Sorry about that... running off like

that... It just all... made me think, you know, it's still..."

He looked up at her. "Melanie," he said. "And my dad..."

Kate could feel the answers so close, could almost see them move on his tongue as he spoke, wanted to reach out and touch them, feel them.

"What?" she asked.

He shook his head slightly. "About my dad," he said. "About him… dying. About the way it happened. What he did. Why he did it. About me."

He'd said it quick, like he'd thought about it over and over, paranoia multiplying inside him. Kate hesitated and tried to speak softly to him. "What do you mean, about you?"

"About everything that happened. Me... and Melanie. I haven't seen her since. She just went, she left town... I mean I presumed she had. No one saw her and she didn't answer my calls or anything... and if she's come back now, of all times, just come back without a word or anything... if Mum finds out she's around... it'll bring it all back again, when she's trying to get over it all. I don't know how she'll cope with that."

"Your mum can cope, better than you think probably. I know it's hard, even though she likes to make it seem like she's fine, that's what she said, coping fine, the note in the Christmas card said, besides, your mum thought Melanie was still here anyway…" She stopped. Wished she could strip those moments away, take the words back. He was staring at her.

"What note? What Christmas card? What do you mean?"

Kate held onto her bottom lip with her teeth for a moment. She felt the skin on her face begin to itch and burn.

"Well, your mum sent a card with a note in it, for Melanie, to tell her about it."

He didn't say anything for a moment, just stared at her, his face washed with some kind of pain. "Melanie told you that?" he asked. "What do you mean? Sent a card where?"

Kate thought briefly about holding onto the slippery end of this lie. She looked at Anthony and for a moment felt sorry for him. He looked vulnerable. She didn't really want to weigh him down with another lie.

"No," she hesitated. "Melanie didn't tell me. I mean, your mum sent the card to the flat, so she obviously thought Melanie still lived there."

"To your flat? Is that what you mean?"

Kate could feel all the little lies overlapping and worming away in her muscles and veins. It was becoming too confusing, too hard to understand and decipher just what she should and shouldn't say. She could hear her voice coming out much quieter than before, afraid to speak it too loudly, hoping it would be softer and easier to take like this. "Yes," she said. "But, of course Melanie wasn't there, so I opened it."

"You opened it? I don't understand. You're her friend. You must have known all along where she was."

"Well, not exactly."

"Not exactly? What's going on, Kate?"

The way he used her name, for the first time, hit her chest hard. He had his father's voice when he said her name, the emphasis on the "t", his head dipping slightly when her name spilled out of his mouth.

"I'm not exactly her friend," she said. "Melanie. I mean, I don't know her as well as I might have made out."

He sat back in his chair, still looking at her. She tried to make out what was going on his head, behind his eyes. "Go on," he said.

"I live in the flat she used to live in, and we've met."

"You've met? When did you meet?"

She couldn't tell him everything. It was too much. She'd have to drip this out and hope he could take it. "Yesterday," she said. "But I knew who she was... I mean, your mum sent the card with the note in about your dad, about Peter."

"Melanie didn't get the card, did she?"

"No."

She watched him. Tried to figure his thoughts, his emotions. Did he hate her now? She couldn't blame him if he did. But he didn't understand, maybe if he knew....

She watched him and waited for him to turn his face on

her.

"But why?" he asked. "Why go to all this trouble pretending you know her?"

Kate shrugged. Still couldn't tell him the truth. "I don't know," she said. "I just wanted to be… part of something, and your family seemed so… nice."

Anthony let a small laugh go, his shoulders moving forward in a mock shrug. "Nice?" he said. "My family aren't nice." He was staring down at the carpet around his feet under the table. He shook his head. "But it doesn't matter," he said. "None of it really matters."

Kate felt a strange relief run in her veins and her body. She'd let one of them go, but still kept the wedged-in secrets, some moving, some still. She waited for a few minutes, then she said, "What now? What happens now?"

"I don't know what happens now," he said. "I don't even know why Melanie's here. If she went all that way to get away, why has she come straight back?"

"Because of Peter," Kate said. "Why else?"

*

Matthew put the Playstation controller aside and turned his head. He could hear someone knocking hard on the door downstairs. He frowned and stood up. No one ever came to the flat. Only people selling things and the window cleaner wanting to be paid. He ran down and opened the door. A woman stood there. About sixty he guessed. He stared at her.

"Sorry to bother you," she said, "but is Kate in?"

Matthew frowned. "Kate?" he said. "No, she's out at her mum's."

The woman looked disappointed. "Oh," she said. "Well maybe you can help me. It's about Melanie."

Matthew's frown deepened. "Who?" he asked.

"Melanie. The woman who lived here before Kate did. Only I know they are friends and…"

Matthew shook his head slightly so that his hair swayed like a wet dog's fur. "Sorry," he said. "Who are friends?"

"Melanie and Kate. Kate told us at the funeral they were friends. It didn't surprise me at all that Melanie didn't come, but… Anyway, the thing is I was hoping to contact Melanie and I thought Kate would know where she is."

Matthew just looked at her.

"So, do you know if she has a phone number, or address or anything?" the woman said.

Matthew felt his cheeks become hot and fill with blood. "I… I don't know," he said. "Shall I get her to contact you so she can tell you herself?"

"Yes please," the woman went on. "If you wouldn't mind. Everything has been such chaos since Peter died, so this one thing would be a great help to me."

"Yes," Matthew said. "Sure." He hesitated, then said, "Peter was your…?" He let the question hang, but she knew what he was asking.

"My husband," the woman said.

Matthew nodded. "Sorry," he muttered.

"That's OK," she said. "Just tell Kate that Susie was here, would you, and if she could pass on those details about Melanie, I would be ever so grateful."

Matthew nodded again, his speech lost somewhere in the last words of the conversation. Peter had a wife, a family. Of course he did, but Matthew hadn't thought of any of that before. It was like none of that existed if he couldn't see it. If he didn't make himself think of it. He slowly closed the door and sat down on the bottom of the stairs. A weight like water in a sack pulled deep in his body.

*

"It wasn't your fault," she said. "About your dad."

"How do you know? You don't know that."

"I know because... I never told you before, I know I

should have, but I'm telling you now, I'm trying to be up front and honest with you now." She could feel him staring at her, waiting, his breath held back a little, coming out thinly, his nerves tensing, worry about what she was going to say. She could feel everything stop and the moment quiet and strained. Waiting. "I knew Peter," she said. "Your dad. I knew him. I work at the rope factory, I worked with him… I didn't know Melanie, but I knew Peter."

He was quiet at first, like all the things she'd said were jostling for a position inside him and he couldn't figure where they should go. Then he said, "I don't know why you would lie."

"I didn't lie, I just didn't..."

"Come on," he interrupted. "It's the same thing, you know that."

"I came to the funeral to... say goodbye, to... make peace, but when I got there it all felt wrong, like I shouldn't have been there."

"What do you mean?"

"I mean, people were talking, saying no one was supposed to have come from the factory and..."

"No," he said, shaking his head. "I mean about making peace, what did you mean when you said you wanted to make peace? What for?"

"Him... dying. I..."

He was staring at her now.

"But I didn't want to burden any of you with all that. It seemed like an intrusion," she said. "Like my... issues were nothing compared to yours, to his family's."

"Issues?"

Kate could feel the discomfort running all over her. Him watching her too closely, trying to understand her through her skin and her movements and every gesture she made. "I've been off work," she said. "With stress. I've found it hard."

He narrowed his eyes, then he nodded slightly. "It was a shock," he said. "If you worked with him, I can see how it would have been."

She looked up at him, leaned forward slightly. "Yes,"

she said. "It was a shock."

"But that still doesn't explain why you lied about it all, made up stories and shit."

She looked down again. "I'm sorry."

She looked like she might cry then. Could feel it inside her. Anthony never did like to see girls cry. "It's OK," he said. "I actually think it helps. And I mean for both of us, I think, at least we can talk about it, with each other. It's good to have a friend."

He turned to look at her, his arms wrapped round his knees. "You ever had a friend who wasn't a friend?"

She frowned. "What do you mean?"

"Well, someone you thought was a friend, but who didn't really care about you at all."

Kate tried to nod sympathetically. "But surely you can choose who your friends are…?"

"When I was fifteen dad decided to rent a cottage for our summer holiday and said I could take a friend. My brothers, James and Paul, were pissed off about it because they couldn't bring anyone, but, well, I didn't care. I took these two guys who were my mates then." He realised Kate was looking at him a little blankly now. "You don't know what I'm going on about, do you?"

He started shuffling around as if he was about to stand up.

"No, no," she insisted. "You bought the drinks when we got here. Let me buy a round. Another pint?"

*

There had been a moment at school, just one lunch time, just half an hour or so, when everything had changed for Anthony. He was thirteen coming up fourteen. Stuart Mace passed him on their way out of the school doors. He clipped the side of Anthony's skull with his flat palm. Anthony ducked his head and tried not to make eye contact. Stuart Mace still wouldn't leave him alone, not even now he'd lost the extra weight he once carried and did his best to stay out of the boy's way. Still Anthony was the target.

Easy. Familiar. Safe.

"Come on, Tony," Stuart said. Anthony winced at the unwanted use of his shortened name. Looked up at the other boy.

"Over the road," he went on, pointing across from the school where a bridge stretched over the river. "I've got something for you to do."

Anthony didn't answer, just looked at him.

"Well, come on then," Stuart said, and he grabbed the shoulder of Anthony's coat and pulled him forward.

That day, over the road from the school, by the river, under the bridge, Anthony had stepped forward. He'd watched while Stuart untied the rope that was tied firmly around the branches of the tree. The rope that was always left there and that Anthony had played on endlessly, swinging over the ditch. Stuart had untied lengths of the rope then chose the one that would best serve them.

"See that kid?" he said. He put his arm around Anthony and pointed to a boy up ahead.

"Yeah."

"I want you to take this and go up behind him and..." he pulled the rope suddenly in his hands and clenched his jaw. "Round his scrawny neck."

He held the rope out to Anthony.

"Go on then," Stuart said.

Anthony hesitated, glanced at Stuart.

"What?"

"Strangle him."

Seriously? Stuart was telling him to strangle someone. The boy stood with his back to Anthony. He was talking to a friend, but they both looked so harmless. Stuart pushed the rope into Anthony's arms and gave him a hard shove. "Go on," he said. "That little git's been mouthing off about me. Thinks he's clever. Well, we'll see who's so bloody clever. Go on. Somebody's got to do it."

Anthony had to do it. That much was obvious. There was no escape route that he could see. He looked around. Two or three other boys stood with their hands in their pockets. Waiting. There was no other way.

"Do it," Stuart said. "Or do you want me to just strangle you instead?"

So Anthony walked quickly up behind the boy. He moved fast, partly so the boy wouldn't get spooked and partly because, if he did this quickly there was less time to think about what he was doing. Just do it. He stopped behind the boy, swiftly hooked the looped rope over his head and held the rope around the boy's windpipe. He pulled tightly until the boy was heavy and fell to the ground. Stuart was laughing and pointing down at the boy. "Fucking brilliant," he said. "He fell in a pile of dog shit or something."

Anthony felt like the air around his head was closing in on him. His world was getting smaller. He couldn't see the fields anymore, couldn't hear the other kids back in the yard at school, couldn't feel if the weather was warm or cold or wet today. The boy who he'd choked was back on his feet before Anthony started to become aware again. At first he looked totally shocked, stumbling back into his friend. Then he was cursing and shouting about the shit that was hung in clumps on his clothing where he'd collapsed into it on the ground. Stuart was still laughing. "That was fucking brilliant, man," he said. And he patted Anthony's shoulder hard so that Anthony's body jolted forward a little. "Mate," Stuart said, nodding his head and looking Anthony full in the face. "That was really fucking cool."

It was some kind of release.

He was sitting in his room back at home after school, crying. But it was like throwing up when you've seen something shocking. There was no actual physical reason why he should be doing it. It just had to come out. For a second, under that bridge, by that river over the road from school, he thought he'd killed that boy. He couldn't remember actually thinking it, but the thought must have been forming somewhere in his brain: *I've killed him. Shit, I've killed him.* Because he could have killed him, couldn't he? That's why Stuart picked him to do it. Stuart wouldn't get his hands dirty. Stuart wouldn't nearly kill a boy, would he?

The strange thing was, weirdly, worryingly, the whole episode seemed to have made Anthony cooler. Stuart had clapped him on the back, called him "mate", smiled at him and looked him in the eyes.

Anthony wasn't sure if he was supposed to feel a blast of pride about this. But he did all the same.

He can hear his father's words still.

"Pull yourself together boy!"

Anthony had been crying. He'd made it home from school that day and he'd closed his bedroom door. But everyone in the house could hear him. They all knew he was crying. Although he didn't tell them why.

His father said the words with disgust laced right through them. He pushed Anthony's bedroom door open and he stepped inside. Anthony looked up once, then away again. Peter didn't understand. He told Anthony so. Anthony was weak. Needed to toughen up. Needed to pull himself together. Needed to stand up for himself more.

And then the school called.

Susie took the call of course. It's one of those things men don't do in the house, answering the phone, along with putting away clothes and arranging cushions and ornaments. There's no logical explanation that he can think of, it's just something that women do more of than men. He only ever answered the phone if he was home alone or no one else had answered it and he felt he had to. Was he afraid, always, of who might be on the other end? Were all men afraid of conversations and communication with unknown individuals they couldn't see?

Susie answered the call, and Peter didn't think anything of it until she came quietly into the living room and stood by the sofa, her hands overlaying each other, and she waited for him to look up and notice.

"What's the matter?" he asked. He felt, as he looked at her, that he didn't want to hear this. Wished as soon as he'd asked that he'd never had to.

"That was the school," she answered. "It's about Anthony."

"What about Anthony?"

"He's been in some trouble. They want us to go in so they can have a chat with us."

A chat. Why do people make it sound so cosy? A chat. It was something Susie would have with her sister if she had one. Something his mother would have had with hers. It wasn't the kind of thing parents had with head teachers when they'd been called in over trouble their son was in.

The school seemed a soulless place to Peter. Empty and quiet with an after-hours at the pub feel to it. Like he shouldn't be there. Like no one should. Maybe just the landlord because he lived there. Maybe just the head because they had to be.

He walked down the corridor with Susie and he couldn't shift that stupid feeling of guilt. Walking down a school corridor towards the head's office. Still felt the same. After all these years. Even now he was an adult. Even though he'd nothing to feel guilty about...

He took a glance at Susie, all calm and respectable, and then he suddenly realised he did feel it. He felt the guilt shoot inside him.

He'd promised. Stupid promises you make when you're young. But he'd promised. What were the words? *Forsaking all others*. Had he truly *forsaken* all others? What did that mean, anyway? No looking at pretty girls? No flirting? Was it something that was possible for any human being?

He looked at Susie until she felt it and turned to look back at him. He could see the worry on her face, the confusion and the disbelief over Anthony, but no guilt.

Even so, it wouldn't go away. The closer they got to the headmaster's room, the more the feeling of guilt kept on creeping over Peter's skin. Stupid. Should a father feel guilt for his son's crimes? But Peter felt plenty of it. Just like being a kid again. Dread puthered inside him as they reached the door. They sat in the small office with the head teacher on the other side of the desk, looking down at some notes, looking up at them through his varifocal glasses, looking down again, his eyes appearing at once large then normal then small.

It was a very serious business, the head teacher told them. There had been an incident. Susie took a lung full of breath in at the word "incident".

"What incident?" Peter demanded. "And what has it got to do with us?"

"It's regarding Anthony," he said. "Yes, there's been some trouble, I'm afraid. There's been an accusation."

Accusation. Peter rolled the word around on his tongue, while at the same time feeling the anger take hold of his insides and squeeze. "If this is something to do with that bloody bully..." He pointed at no one, nothing in particular. "You know our Anthony's life's been made a misery by that bloody bully."

Susie turned in her seat and stared at him in amazement. Anthony really had been bullied and the pair of them had kept it all from her, wrapped it up between them and dealt with it in their own little way. Susie felt the anger at being kept in the dark rise up in her. Peter glanced at her, but the head teacher was talking again.

"I'm sorry, I'm not aware of any bullying being perpetrated *against* Anthony," he said.

"Are you trying to say my son is the one doing the bullying? Are you calling my son a bully?" He knew his voice was getting louder. He knew he'd stood up and that Susie's hand was on his arm and her face was looking up and pleading with him. *Sit down, Peter, please, just sit down.*

But the head teacher just looked down then up again, his eyes doing a strange magic trick that unnerved Peter. "I don't know anything about that, but there's been an accusation made against Anthony."

The head teacher breathed evenly and closed his eyes for a second. When he opened them he spoke again. "I'm not calling anyone a bully, but there is an accusation that I must take very seriously. After all, it could have been very serious indeed. Someone could have died."

"And what actually is this 'accusation'?"

"There was an incident after school and a boy was strangled with a rope. The boy lost consciousness for a time. I'm afraid his parents have made a complaint and I have to follow it up. They have told me they are considering reporting it to the police."

He did what a good parent should do. Did what any father would have done. He went straight home to tell Anthony it was time to grow up. Time to take responsibility. Anthony could cry as much as he liked but Peter didn't care. He had to realise that if he went around doing stupid things like that there would have to be consequences. He didn't feel any pity for the boy. He'd done a stupid thing. No pity. Just disappointment. He felt something shrivel inside him. How could he have brought up a son like that?

Peter made the call he knew he had to make to the parents of the boy. The boy Anthony had... attacked. It still seemed unbelievable to Peter. It still felt like it couldn't have been *his* son who did this. What went wrong? He just couldn't add it all up and get to this.

He told the parents there'd been some problems at home. A lie, though the more he spoke it and heard his own words, and the more he thought about it, the more it seemed to be true. There were problems at home. At least there were now.

"I'm just ringing to ask you, to appeal to you really, please don't take this any further. Please. Anthony, he's not a bad boy, he's never been in any trouble before, and I promise you, he's dealing with the consequences of his actions now, believe me, his mother and I, we won't let him off with this, believe me, but please, give him a chance, I promise nothing like this will ever happen again and he is truly sorry for what he's done."

Peter felt he'd hardly taken in any breath at all while he spoke. Then he waited. There was a pause on the other end of the line, followed by the mother of the boy saying she'd thought about it.

"I just hope you, and he, realise how serious this is."

"Of course," Peter replied.

"Your boy could have killed him, for goodness' sake."

"I know, I'm..."

"Not to mention the trauma this has caused, the anxiety, he's very upset."

"And I can't apologise enough for my son's behaviour, but... please," Peter said. "I'm begging you. He deserves another chance."

The woman paused again and then said, slowly, "OK... I'm prepared to take it no further. This time, but if anything..."

"I can promise you nothing like this will happen again. You have my word."

When Peter laid the phone back down next to the framed photos on the sideboard in the hallway, he felt his body slump. He'd never been so humiliated. Begging the woman to let this lie. He stood there in the hallway for a few minutes. He knew he'd had to do it, but he'd never felt such a loss of pride before. What must that woman think of him? Begging her like that, pleading with her. For Anthony. Anthony who'd caused all this trouble and who didn't seem to realise just what he'd done.

"What were you thinking?" his dad said.

Anthony couldn't stop crying even though he wanted to.

"Don't you realise how strong rope is? It doesn't just snap, you know! It's tough, sturdy… reliable. Not like you!"

Anthony managed to hold back his sobbing enough to shout out. "But this was all your fault in the first place!"

"My fault?"

"You told me to hit him. Stuart. You said if he was bullying me I should hit him. So I did. That's how all this started!"

"You needed to toughen up! It was good for you to learn how to defend yourself properly, instead of being such a wimp!"

"But don't you see? The only reason he doesn't beat me up anymore is because I jump to all his commands and do everything he tells me. He's never ever going to leave me alone!

That's why I had to strangle that boy," Anthony spluttered. "I was doing it for him. And whatever you say, that's all your fault!"

Neither of them said anything for a minute. Then Anthony heard a sigh. Full of disappointment.

"You could have killed him," was all his dad kept saying. Over and over. "You could have killed him." Until the words slipped in Anthony's brain and it began to sound like it had been an option. He could have killed him. But he didn't.

*

He's 15. Sitting with two mates talking. Sitting at a bar on holiday, drinking Coke, feeling big.

"Do you remember when you strangled that kid…?"

Anthony looks uneasily at Stuart. "Yeah," he says. "That was mad."

Stuart sits up straight. "Funny though, wasn't it?" he says. "And it's all a bit boring round here. We should make things more interesting. Try this out." Stuart holds up a metal-chain dog leash, hanging from his fist like an executioner's rope.

Anthony lets go an awkward laugh. "Yeah, right," he says. "Where'd you get that anyway?"

He shrugs. "Cottage owner's dog, you know, that big bastard that barks next door."

"What, you took that off the dog without getting your hand bitten off?"

"Yeah, not a big deal. So let's have some fun."

Anthony leans his body away from his friend. "Well, you're not coming anywhere near me with that."

They all laugh and take another sip of their drinks. It's Cornwall in summer. Not much to do unless you were old enough to go out drinking, which they weren't. James and Paul went round the pubs every night, Anthony noticed, and he'd asked them if him and his mates could tag along, but his brothers had just laughed at him. "No chance," James had said, "we don't want a bunch of kids hanging round with us."

So they were making their own entertainment.

*

Stuart is swinging the dog chain a bit in his seat. Then all of a sudden he is fast with it as he loops it over Anthony's head, just how Anthony had done with the rope and that boy that time outside school. Anthony's hands instinctively go up and separate the leash from his neck, just before the metal imprints itself on his flesh. Stuart is laughing, but pulling hard with the leash. They tussle for a moment, and Anthony feels a well of panic rise in him. Then Stuart lets his grip go and the leash falls and slithers over Anthony's arm and chest. Anthony knows a blush has entered his face and he's still holding his hands near his neck. But Stuart has turned away and is nudging the kid at the other side of him. "See his face?" he says. "He thought I was really gonna do it!"

The other kid is laughing hard, too hard Anthony thinks, probably because he's glad it wasn't him with a dog leash round his neck. Probably because he knows he could be next.

Anthony slowly finds his hands returning to his drink on the bar, his body relaxing a little. He chances a look at the other two and he grins at them. What a lark. What a joke.

Anthony had been quiet that afternoon. It was just a joke, he knew that, Stuart wouldn't really have done it, not really, but still. It reminded him of who he was, and he supposed that was part of the purpose of it. Though he didn't kid himself that Stuart was aware of that, he didn't think for one minute that Stuart was intelligent enough to know that was part of why he did it. Anthony knew. And it made him feel lost all over again. Just like when it all first started. Just like when Stuart had started out by calling him names and shoving him around. It took Anthony right back there.

He'd made an excuse about not feeling well and Stuart had shrugged. "No worries," he'd said. "I'm sure we can have our own fun without you."

And the two of them had walked away. Anthony had noticed right then that Stuart still had that metal dog leash in his hand, still swinging it by his legs, but Anthony never thought much of that at the time.

It had been late when Anthony heard about it. The afternoon sun was dying and a breeze swept slowly through the air. Anthony was sitting with them outside on the patio. Neither of them asked about earlier when he'd said he was ill and he didn't ask much either. Just looked around for the dog leash and saw that they didn't have it anymore.

"So where'd you go?" Anthony asked.

The two boys sniggered and looked at each other.

"Oh just around," Stuart said.

And that was it. But it was enough.

The owner of the cottage came round that evening, and came out onto the patio with Anthony's dad. "Don't suppose you boys know anything about some trouble at Windsurf Bar."

Anthony looked sharply at the man. "Trouble?" but the other two kept quiet and just shook their heads.

"Yeah," the man said. "Looks like they've been done over."

"Robbed?"

"Well, no, there wasn't any money in there. It's how the place has been smashed up, though, that's the thing."

Anthony looked at the other two. They weren't saying anything, just staring at the table. Anthony noticed how their feet fidgeted and he knew they'd done it.

The owner knew as well, though he couldn't prove it.

Peter didn't even argue with the guy, just looked at Anthony as if he could never, no matter what he did, be more disappointed in him than he was now.

Peter had called the parents of the other two boys to tell them he was bringing them home early. Stuart had shrugged and said

Peter could say what he liked, no one could prove he'd done a thing and he'd just deny it. So Peter drove them all the way to Lyme. It was late when he got back to the house in Cornwall.

Anthony had gone to bed, but Peter knew he wouldn't be asleep and he went into the dark room. He didn't sit down on the edge of the bed, but stood stiffly in the doorway, looking down at his son.

"Anthony," he said. "I know you're awake."

Anthony didn't respond or move at all at first.

"That boy," his dad went on. "Stuart. The one I just took home."

He waited a minute until Anthony stirred in his bed and turned to look at his dad.

"It's the same boy, isn't it?" Peter said. "It's the boy who bullied you and caused you all that trouble. It's that kid who beat you up that time, isn't it?"

Anthony sat up in the bed. "What did you say to him?" he asked.

"I didn't say anything. I could hear the two of them talking in the back of the car. Other one says to him, *It's alright for you, you never get in trouble, no matter what you do,* and I remembered the name. Stuart. It is him, isn't it?"

"What if it is?"

"You'd bring him here? With us? On our holiday? What the hell were you thinking?"

"You wouldn't understand."

"You've got that right. I don't understand you at all. What about the other boy?"

"What about him?"

"Is he a bully too?"

"No. No, he…he just goes along with it… I think. Stuart really doesn't give a toss about anything but he's not like that, he'll be in big trouble for having to go home early… for what's happened. His parents will go mad."

But it was his own fault, Peter was thinking. He shouldn't have done what he did. "Well, maybe it'll teach him a lesson then," he said. Peter spoke more quietly now. "Anyway, it's late, and I don't want any more bother."

If he could have stayed in that bed for the rest of the holiday he would have. Some holiday it would be now. Anthony sat around and waited for it to be over, thinking all the time about what he would face when he got home. What Stuart would say and do. The threat squeezed him and tensed every inch of him tight. And while he was still here, waiting for the inevitable, his two brothers smirked and called him a loser, and seemed to be having the time of their lives.

*

"I was bullied when I was between twelve and about fourteen. Because I was a bit of a geek I suppose."

Kate turned quickly to look at him, a smile widening on her face. "You were a geek? How do you mean?"

"Yeah, I suppose I was an easy target. I was always quite shy and Mum was a bit... well, she used to take me right to the school gates long after all the other boys were walking to school on their own. I suppose it was with me being the youngest, you know, the baby of the family, but anyway, you know what kids are like, and I got picked on because of it. Add to that the fact that I was a bit... nerdy, and well... I'm not saying that's an excuse, but, well, maybe it goes some way to explaining."

He stopped to check on her reaction. She wasn't saying anything. She was just staring out at the ocean. She glanced at him once to see why he'd stopped. He moved some hair away from his eye and touched his beard. She was thinking about the rope at home.

"But it's awful," she said. "He half-strangled you on your holiday?"

The rope Matthew had brought into the house and that had caused a subdued argument and now lay in a lethargic curl on the furniture like a mischievous, spoilt cat.

She looked at Anthony with sympathy.

It seemed like the most understanding look anyone had ever given him in his whole life. He nodded. And he thought about what a terrible thing it was that he had done to that other kid. What would she have said about that?

"My life was a misery back then," he said. "And there didn't seem to be any way out of it. This kid, Stuart, he bullied me at the start of secondary school cause I was a 'mummy's boy' or whatever, but it didn't stop when I'd started walking to school on my own, I suppose it was too late by then, it was like he had already sized me up and it didn't matter what I did, it wouldn't make any difference. I actually ended up being part of his gang, sort of, you know, I ended up hanging round with him, we were *friends*. Though, of course, I know he was never really my friend. He just wanted someone he could boss around."

He stopped for a minute and looked at her.

She realised she hadn't been paying attention. She was still thinking about the rope, weighing it up against Matthew to see which was heaviest. Deciding Matthew would never hurt her. That she trusted him. Knew he would never hurt anyone.

"It's funny how that happens, isn't it?" he was continuing. "He made my life a misery and yet I still hung around with him and called him my mate."

Kate was frowning at him. "Why?" she said.

"Cos... I didn't have any other friends. Cos being his friend made me cool. I don't know, cos I didn't feel I really had any choice I suppose. It was like, if I didn't do what he said, be his friend, what would he do? He'd give me another kicking, only worse than before. Who knows what he was capable of? It was only when I met Melanie that I felt I was inside my own skin again and felt comfortable being myself, and that somebody loved me for who I actually am. She saved me from my hell of having no friends of my own."

Kate nodded. She suddenly wondered if she truly felt she could be herself when she was with Matt. Was that what love was all about?

"Anyway, letting Melanie get away was the most stupid of all the things I did. I'm a fucking idiot." He shook his head. "My dad thought of me as a real disappointment to him, I know he did, though it wasn't fair. I tried, you know, I wanted to make him happy, make him proud even, it just never worked out that way. And Melanie was the only one... until – well, it became awkward for her with my dad, and she chose to give up on me because of that. So obviously I never meant as much to her as I thought."

She didn't know what to say. He could feel the absence of any words, any sounds at all, becoming heavier in the air between them. But he couldn't blame her. What was she supposed to say to that? Probably thought he was a complete freak now.

Maybe it was pity that drove her, maybe she felt sorry for him now and wanted to do something, say something, give him something. That's what he thought. But it wasn't pity. She didn't feel sorry for him. She was just seeing him as a real person now, not a younger version of Peter, not an altered ghost, but an individual person. She felt a surge of caring. By telling her these things, these moments from his life, these bubbles of time, he had made her care, and she didn't like the idea of lying now. He'd given her some truths, he didn't have to do that, but he had. She would give him something back.

"It wasn't your fault," she said. "You were just a kid, besides it's not as if you were the one who decided to do those things, you were bullied into it."

"Everyone's got a choice," he said. "You can do the right thing if you want to. I didn't."

"But, it's not connected to what your dad did."

He shrugged. Pulled at a thread on his sleeve.

"Listen, I've got Melanie's address if you want it..."

He looked her in the face quickly. She knew that, for that moment, he couldn't decide if it was a good idea or not.

"If you want," she went on. "I mean, it's up to you."

"I don't know," he said. "Me and Mel, and everything."

"It just seems to me that, while she's here, you should... talk to her. She'll leave again soon and the chance is gone. I think you should."

"Some things are better left alone."

"I think you'll regret it if you don't." Then she sat back in her chair. "But that's just what I think. I've got her address at home though, if you want it, I can nip in and get it."

He was staring at the wood of the table. Then he began nodding slowly. He picked up his pint and downed the beer fast. Then he stood up and pushed his chair back behind him. "OK, come on," he said. "Before I change my mind."

*

Up in the flat Matthew is looking out of the window. He hasn't been waiting for her, he assures himself, but it's getting late and she's been gone hours. He touches the curtain and leans forward. There's always people in the street. Sometimes Matthew hates living in a place like this. Tourists think it's so perfect, so relaxing, so calm, so *picturesque.* They should try actually living here. Summer's the worst, of course, but in winter, especially around Christmas, you still get packs of families renting out holiday lets. He could see some of them now, wandering slowly through the narrow street down there, stopping to look in windows and dream of how lovely it must be to live here. Dream on, he thinks.

He's about to move away from the window when he sees them. He's quite a bit taller than her and, as they walk along the thin street, she looks up at him while he talks to her. Matthew can see her face upturned in the light from a window as they slowly walk on. She isn't smiling, just listening as the guy talks. The guy is looking down at her face, then he looks to the ground and seems to be watching his own feet as he walks.

*

She paused and the weight of the words she was about to speak almost stopped time dead.

A pair of boy racers tried to outdo each other in the thin streets, jolting to a stop at the traffic lights and revving their engines, impatient, frustrated in their box-like cars. They were off the moment the lights patted from red to a slow amber.

She took his hands in hers and looked him in the eyes. It wasn't just that she wanted to give him Melanie's address. There was something else she could give him too, something that she needed to get off her chest.

Her heart was beating faster and her breathing became heavy. "Anthony... what happened," she said, "what he did, wasn't your fault. It has nothing to do with *this*. I know it wasn't your fault because it was mine."

*

Matthew leans closer to the window. He can't see the guy's face properly, has no idea who this is, but he hates him. He turns away from the window quickly, walking fast to the back door, down the stairs, and out into the cold evening air.

So this was it? This was it all along?

Matthew kept his distance for a minute. He could feel something building inside him. He'd been angry about the funeral and he knew she was withholding things from him, but he hadn't had any proof he could confront her with. It was just little things, things she shut him off from, new clothes for a funeral that should have nothing to do with her. He'd been angry before, but not like this. Now he had proof. He was looking right at it.

The man was a lot taller than Kate, taller than Matthew, he could see that as he followed them down past the pub. He was tall and skinny. Matthew felt his hands tense by his sides as he walked. They'd been speaking to each other all the way as they walked, God knows what about, and now they walked.

*

Anthony's mind ran through all these things. Kate. Peter. Melanie. What Kate had just said was ridiculous. Didn't make any sense. He pushed it down and compacted it tightly in his head. That was crazy. She knew him. She worked with him. How could it have been her fault? Then Melanie. So, she must have worked with Melanie too, or known her there. So Melanie had gone to Portugal. For a moment that idea was too big for him to fit it comfortably inside him. It covered everything else. Maybe he made it cover everything else. She'd moved away, to another country. Was it really that bad? He suddenly felt completely alone. The only woman he'd ever trusted, conspiring behind his back and leaving him alone. Not even telling him where she'd gone or that she'd gone at all. And this woman. Kate. Manipulating him. Getting him into a situation, get him to talk, get him to listen, make him confess.

He looked up as he became aware of a figure appearing out from an alleyway and striding into the narrow street. He could feel Kate tense beside him as she too saw the movement of a person heading their way.

He came right up to them, and Anthony looked the man in the face. He knew him. It had been some time, years in fact, since he'd seen him, but he'd know him anywhere.

He was slightly shorter than Anthony, but stockier. Stockier than he'd been at school. He had his head tilted backwards slightly so that he looked at Anthony from under his eyelids, even though Anthony was the taller of the two of them. He looked at him with a certainty, as if he knew things about Anthony and would use them against him now.

"What's going on?" Matthew said.

Kate was standing beside Anthony now, staring straight back at him as he approached. At least she was no longer holding his hand, he noticed.

Anthony frowned a minute and mumbled. "I'm just..."

Then he grinned and flapped his arms out by his sides. Joker.

"Well," Matthew said. "I'm telling you. Back off."

Anthony frowned again, but only for a second before Matthew pushed him backwards. Matthew felt his anger released from his body as Anthony stumbled.

This was what she'd been up to. This was really it? This? With this loser? The sight of this guy sprawled on the ground filled Matthew with a strange kind of disgust. She would sneak around with this idiot? He looked at him, then he hauled him up from the ground by his stupid denim jacket and shoved him against the wall.

Matthew didn't give up. Even though Kate was screaming at him to stop, it just got worse, despite Anthony managing to get a couple of flailing punches in. He supposed he should feel something, some kind of satisfaction in that, but he didn't. There was no slow motion now, not like that day at school when he'd punched Stuart. There was only a desperate scramble.

Matthew kept pushing him. Scuffling and squaring up to him, trying to make himself seem as tall as Anthony.

But Anthony had that one advantage over Matthew, his height, and he knew he could use it now. He forced himself around Matthew and laid his whole weight into him to get him to the ground. It was a messy, scrappy manoeuvre and they ended up in a heap, Matthew's rage tearing at him from beneath to try to dislodge him. Anthony was thinking that if he could just manage to keep Matthew down he might be able to get into a sitting position on top of him.

It was only then that Anthony realised where they were. This was where Melanie used to live. If he hadn't stopped in his tracks there, his body heavy, his brain invaded by sudden thoughts of Melanie and the flat she lived in, the way she'd left his life and never said goodbye, if he hadn't been looking up at the window of the flat above him now, he would have been able to jump up and get away from Matthew.

What did he think he was doing? He was looking up at their flat. The bastard. Rage surged through Matthew and he grappled his ex-classmate to the floor. As they both tried to be the first one to get to their feet Matthew noticed him turn and look at Kate. Did he think she'd help him? Matthew knew she wouldn't. He knew that, didn't he? He knew Kate better than anyone else alive. He knew everything there was to know about her. Inside out. How easily she bruised. Where she did and didn't like to be touched. The things she was and wasn't prepared to talk about. How thin her wrists were. How small her waist was.

Kate could hardly bear to watch. Matthew did an odd ducking motion, like a pro boxer, like a dip in a lie detector. He shook his hair from his face and pushed Anthony hard on the shoulder as he straightened up. Anthony stumbled, one foot struggling for a moment to find its place on the ground again. And the gloves were off. Matthew prepared his body and he rammed it hard into Anthony.

Kate put her hands up to her mouth, involuntarily, like a rush of water straight from a pipe. She heard her breath pulled quickly up into her throat. For a moment she felt as if she couldn't move. Against the wall of the opposite house, Kate could see how much thinner Anthony was. He surely didn't stand a chance against Matthew. The two men were locked into each other for a moment. Their arms encircled, tensed, their muscles defined by shadows as they scuffled and tried to take hold of the fight again. Matthew must have managed a low punch because he stood back slightly, looked as if he was saying something to Anthony, looked as if he might just power forward and hit him again. Kate couldn't see Anthony's face now, his head bent, his arms around his middle.

She could see the moonlight touching Matthew's hair as he stood waiting for Anthony to answer him or just move, even try to hit him, but do something.

"What are you doing?" she shouted.

Matthew turned and held his hand out behind his body towards her. "Stay out of it, Kate," he said.

She could see dark patches on his knuckles, his skin gritty where it had stretched and split. Blood drying the colour of a garnet.

"Stay out of it? What the hell do you think you're doing? Stop it! Just stop it!"

He half turned his face to her and she saw a slight swell in his bottom lip. "Just don't get involved. This is between me and him," he said.

"Come on," Anthony said. "She's upset."

"You!" Matthew shouted. "Of all people, it had to be you!"

She could see Anthony looking up at her now, one side of his mouth dark like Matthew's hand, blood spilt and drying already till it looked like old, dirty, tarnished copper. "Tell him," he said. "It's not what he thought. There was nothing..." He was shaking his head.

Kate took a step forward and took hold of Matthew's arm from behind him. She lowered her voice. "Matthew, come inside," she said.

He shook her hand off roughly. Still stood with his back to her. Couldn't turn. Couldn't look at her. He stared ahead at Anthony, anger in every inch of him, then he stepped forward again and went to pull Anthony back onto his feet. Kate was right behind him, moving her body with his, pulling at his arm and shouting, "Stop it, Matthew, stop it!" He didn't seem to hear her, and though she moved forward and looked him right in his face, he didn't seem to see her either.

He had hold of Anthony again. Had pulled him up by his coat and was holding him right there. Kate looked to Anthony and saw his eyes flit. His face was close to Matthew's and he stayed calm, saying, "Come on, you're upsetting her."

Matthew didn't move for a moment, just stared into Anthony's face, his fists tight around his coat, his breathing tensed and difficult through his nose and his set mouth.

"Look at her," Anthony went on. "She's upset."

Matthew still held Anthony, but turned his face to see Kate. She was crying, and she hadn't really felt it, hadn't really realised it was happening till Anthony pointed it out.

Matthew was the centre of a wheel. He was in charge of this situation. He could swing it, however he liked. The decision lay with him, turn and walk away, walk back into the flat with Kate, face her again – or ignore her, stay angry. It was up to him. And yet at the same time, he had no control at all, never did.

He kneed Anthony in the balls as hard as he could, and left him to slump back to the floor. He didn't look at Kate again, and turned and walked to the flat. They heard the door at the bottom of the stairs bang shut as Matthew opened it and slammed it behind him again. They remained there for a moment then. The two of them. Then Anthony got to his feet, back still to the wall, wiped his mouth with the sleeve of his denim jacket. He looked over at Kate.

"Do you two know each other?" she asked.

"Sort of," he answered. Then he waved his hand as if batting the question away. "Can you just give me the address now?"

Kate nodded and turned to go back to the flat. She hesitated at the entrance to the alleyway. Matthew was still angry, she knew, and facing him for this moment when she wasn't giving him her full attention was probably the worst way to do it. But she was stuck between the two of them. She opened the door and went slowly up the stairs.

Matthew was walking from one room to the other. Kate went into the flat, straight into the kitchen, and saw the fruit bowl on the floor, by the wall where he'd picked up the first thing he saw when he walked in and threw it hard.

He was pacing in the bedroom. She could hear him breathing like a horse and knew before she got there that his hands were in tight fists and his muscles were tensed. She walked in and went past him to the wardrobe.

"I don't need this!" he shouted at her. "I don't fucking need this!"

She kept quiet and took out the black file and ducked her hands inside until she found the scrap of paper with Melanie's address on it. Melanie had told Kate she would be at this address for another four days before she flew back to Portugal.

"What the fuck are you doing?" he shouted. "I'm talking to you!"

Kate held the paper tight in her hand. The last time she'd done this had been the day of the funeral, when she had checked the name of the woman whose life she would slip inside of for the day. It was still raw in Kate's mind. A day as vague as a midnight dream. A day she didn't want to think about completely and revisit. A day full of so much pain she had turned it inside out and masked it with a lie so she wouldn't have to admit it and feel it.

She looked up at Matthew, his face full of questions and anger and she murmured, "I won't be a minute."

"Won't be a fucking minute? You're not going back out

there... to *him*!"

"It's not what you think, we're not..."

"Then what the fuck is it? Come on Kate. This whole thing. Me and you." He was twisting around where he stood, as if scared that standing still would make him unable to control his body. "Don't try and tell me you're not going off behind my back with *him*." He pointed out of the window, his face strained with anger. "You certainly haven't been shagging me lately."

"Is that what this is about? Sex? Is that it? You think if I don't feel like sex with you then I must be having it off with someone else?"

"Well, are you?"

She shook her head at him. She could feel her own anger enter her neck and throat and threaten to pour out. She took a deep breath. Couldn't look at him now.

She held the paper out in her hand so he could see it, staring at it herself. "I am going back down there and I'm giving him Melanie's address. That's who he's interested in, Melanie, not me. He's never been interested in me and I've never been interested in him, not in the way you think." She looked up at him once. "Can't believe you would think that."

Then she took the paper and walked back through the flat, and down the stairs to the neon-lit street where Anthony sat on the floor waiting. She handed him the paper.

"Here," she said. "Where she's staying, Melanie. Go and see her."

He took the paper from her hand and looked at her. "How is she?" he asked.

Kate shook her head. "I don't know. I've seen her, and she seems fine, but I don't know..."

He looked so vulnerable sitting on the floor like that. She knelt down next to him in the street.

"I'm sorry," she said. "I'm so sorry, Anthony, I never meant to cause you trouble."

He looked at her. "So, what did you mean to do?"

"It wasn't about you, it was about Peter."

"Why did you say it was your fault? His... death... why did you say that?"

"Because I could have stopped him."

Matthew sat down at the kitchen table, leaned his arms on the table top and lay his head down. He had stayed in position sitting at the table, his arms crossed like a loose plait, his chin resting on his wrist. Kate had started running a bath now. Matthew just sat there, staring at the table top. After about twenty minutes Kate came and stood beside him. He looked up at her. What would they do now? Matthew couldn't figure her thoughts or weigh her emotions. He had no clue. He just looked up at her and waited for her to say something.

Kate reached down to his hand on the table and unfolded it from his other arm. His fingers complied and she felt the softness and the warmth of his skin. He moved towards her, stood up, and she led him away from the table.

"I ran you a bath," she said. "You need to clean your face up, and you'll hurt where you've been hit. The water will help."

He'd gone into the bedroom and Kate imagined him getting undressed, quietly moving to the bathroom and into the water. But instead, he appeared back in the kitchen, still dressed.

Matthew had the rope in his hand. He came towards her.

She looked at him, and glanced at the rope, limp in his hand. She could feel the uncertainty in the air. For the first time ever, Kate felt he was too unpredictable, like maybe she didn't know him at all, and had no idea what he was about to do. "You OK?" she asked.

He didn't speak, just moved nearer to her. He took one end of the rope in each hand and watched as Kate smiled uneasily and took a step backwards.

"What are you doing?" she asked.

He grabbed both of her wrists quickly with the middle of the rope and held it firmly, her hands bound together by the hemp. Then he led her slowly to a chair at the kitchen table, kicked it out a little so that it sat away from the table, and eased

Kate into a sitting position. He was always strong. Never anything she could do in terms of physical strength. But he had never used that against her.

"Matt," she said. "What's going on?"

*

Anthony folded the little piece of paper carefully. He'd read the address six times. Knew the street. Had memorised the house number. Had traced the letters on the page with his eyes, his sight lifting with each curve of the pen, his head moving only centimetres with every dip her hand had made while it quickly scribbled down her name and address. He knew her hands. Knew the way they wrote and moved. Knew the size of them and how they felt when he held them like loose rope ready for a tug of war.

He stood up slowly, a rush of blood to his head, a pain in his middle. He would go and find her right now. Ask her what happened. Ask her why one day they were the only people in the world who understood each other, and then the next day she moved away and never contacted him again.

*

Matthew leaned from one foot to the other in front of her. She could almost see the way this problem was playing in his head. He didn't want to hurt her, she really believed he didn't, but at the same time... something else was taking over. It was as if he knew this was wrong and that she might not easily forgive him, but somehow she could tell he'd reached a point of no return in his frustration and his building anger.

He'd bound her hands behind her, over the back of the chair she sat on. She didn't scream. She'd struggled at first and told him no, she didn't want to do this. She'd thought, stupidly, that this was sexual, that Matt was going to force her, but she knew now that it wasn't. He was angry. And Matthew was never normally angry, not with Kate anyway. It was more of a control thing.

"That's what I want to know," he answered. "What's going on? What's really going on? Not 'stress', not all the usual bollocks, what's really going on?"

She stopped struggling with her hands behind her and she felt a blush reach up her neck onto her face and burn there.

"So what's going on?" he asked.

She just looked at him for a moment.

Matthew shook his head slightly, parts of his hair stuck together with sweat. "I don't mean him, that guy, Anthony, well I do, but I know… if you say it wasn't what I thought, then that's fine, OK, but, so what was it? Who is he to you?"

"Do you know him?" she asked.

"Yeah," he answered. "I know who he is, I know what he's like. But how do you know him?"

"He's Peter's son," she said. "How do you know him?"

Matthew stared at her, his mind turning things over and over. He ignored her question. Why should he answer her questions? He wasn't the one with things to hide here, he wasn't the one who had to answer questions. "You're talking about the guy who died?" he said. "Peter. That guy?"

"Yeah," she said quietly. "That guy."

Matthew was frowning, his eyes narrow while he looked at her. "So who is Peter?" he asked. "Really? Why is all this so important? I mean who the hell was he to you?"

Matthew pushed his hand back through his hair and held it on top of his head for a moment. He tightened his fist around the clod of hair he held. Black brown. So dark it looked like wet earth. He looked down at his feet, still moving on the carpet.

"What are you playing at?" he asked her.

Kate pushed doors open in her brain and tried to decide what he was referring to.

"Why did you do it?" he asked.

That question made things even harder. Maybe he knew everything, but Kate couldn't see how he could. She'd left no clues that she could think of. She tried to move her wrists in the knot of rope behind her back. Her breasts felt ridiculously exposed in front of her. She watched him move and tried to catch his eye, tried to follow his face so she could hold onto it.

"Do what?" she asked quietly.

"You know what," he said.

So it must still be about Anthony then. The way he'd said "you know what" sounded fresh, new, as if this was something that was happening right now, or moments ago, or was ongoing. Something she was *playing at*, as he'd put it.

She spoke softly. "Matthew…" she said. "What's all this? Why have you…?"

He still held his hair on his head and Kate could see his patience drip away from him. He couldn't look at her.

"Just answer me!" he shouted.

"It's not what you think," she said.

"How can it be anything other than what I think?"

"We are friends, that's all."

Matthew banged his own head with the heel of his hand. "No, Kate, you are not friends with these people."

These people? She drew her words in and waited. It wasn't about Anthony then. She wasn't sure anymore.

He held onto the long strands of his own hair that fell over his eyes, and he slowly looked up at her.

"You know I had a woman round here today, asking about a *Melanie*. Your *friend* who lived here before I did."

"What woman?"

"The dead man's wife. Peter. His wife came round here looking for you. She wants you to give her Melanie's new address. Said you and Melanie are the best of friends. Apparently Melanie lived here before we did and you became close friends with her. Have you any idea how stupid I felt?"

Kate bent her head till it almost touched her chin. "I'm sorry," she said.

Matthew's voice sounded like it was blunted on all ends, chopped off, his words hard-edged and metallic. "Sorry?" he shouted. "What the hell are you playing at? You don't know this

Melanie. You just pretended you did. And I know you've been opening her mail. What was it? Did you really want to go to a funeral that much? Isn't life crap enough for you already?"

She thought she would start to cry, but really, she'd cried enough in the past couple of weeks and didn't feel as if there was anything left, so she just sat with her head bent, her chin inches away from her chest, her hands tied behind her back.

"What did you tell her?" she murmured.

"What?"

"Susie, Peter's wife, what did you say when she asked about Melanie?"

She glanced up and Matthew was staring hard at her. "I said I'd tell you to contact her and tell her."

"Can you untie me now, please?" she said, quiet, her head bent till it touched her chest.

Matthew was staring at her. "Just needed to keep you in one place so I could ask you," he said. "Talk to you. Just needed to keep you there for a minute. You won't talk to me. Otherwise, you won't talk to me."

The way he was speaking shocked her, every word seemed to come from somewhere she didn't know. He'd never spoken to her like this before. He was pacing about now, still running his hands in his hair and holding onto his head. He looked like he could explode at any minute. "What the fuck is going on?" he shouted at her. "Tell me this time, just fucking tell me!"

"It's not Anthony," she said. "It's not what you think, it's not that at all."

"Are you seeing someone else?" he shouted. "If it's not Anthony, then who?"

"No," she answered. "I just said. It's not that at all."

Matthew looked at her, his anger filling again and again. He kicked out at the wooden bed frame and held his fists tight. Couldn't look at her for a minute. "You've been lying to me, all this time, you've fucking lied to me."

"I haven't," she pleaded. "I haven't lied."

"Well, you haven't told me everything either, have you?

All that stuff with the funeral. Melanie." He put his face right up close to Kate. "And you haven't answered my question. The dead guy: who was he to you?"

He looked at her now, and she saw how he hated her in that moment.

"I'm sorry," she said. "I'll tell you. I'll tell you everything. But you've got to promise you won't get angry."

He shook his head, his mouth pressed tightly together. "Can't promise you that, Kate."

"But it isn't about me and you," she pleaded. "It's about someone else."

"What someone else? Who?"

"Peter," she said. "The whole thing is about what happened to Peter."

He looked at her accusingly. "So why didn't you tell me about it?"

"Because it's about someone else's life, and their death. It wasn't mine to tell!"

"But you were having an affair with him! Weren't you!"

"No!" she half-shouted, incredulous. "Are you insane? Is that what you think? He was old enough to be my dad! Maybe even my granddad!"

He was silent now, wondering whether she was telling the truth, and thinking about everything he'd done because of what he'd thought he knew.

"At least untie me," she murmured.

He stood and looked at her for a moment, then he walked forward quickly and crouched behind her to untie the rope.

When he released her he walked straight out the door and down the stairs, the door at the bottom banging behind him, a second's worth of daylight air creeping into the flat.

She moves slowly to the window. Touches the damp towel that is cold and heavy with moisture in the bottom, tight on the wooden frame. She leans against the glass. Down in the close street she can see Matthew. He is sitting on the curb, by a dip between two houses across the road. He is holding onto the toes of his shoes with his fingertips, bending his feet inwards towards his knees. At first Kate thinks he is staring into the road, but then she realises he is looking down, maybe at the stones between the old cobbles, maybe at nothing at all. His hair is swept over, thick dark brown, almost black, making S shapes by his ears. She can't see his eyes, but a slight frown is worrying his head above them. He doesn't glance upwards at all. She can see his cheeks heavy. His mouth in what looks like a sulk – but Kate knows it isn't.

He is thinking over what he has just done, and what Kate did. He is trying to make some sort of sense of it all. Trying to figure it.

He is thinking over what might happen next.

She stands there for a little while. After what he just did, she has no idea how to follow, no clue as to where she can go from here. She stands at the window and touches the damp towel on the ledge, soaked in condensation and rainwater that has seeped in like a hand pushing under clothing, pushing forward to touch skin. She glances behind her at the Christmas tree, its prickly branches reaching out into the room. It looks like it's trying to escape from the heavy shroud of tinsel wrapped around it, holding out its hands to be saved. She turns back and looks at Matthew again, still sitting in the street, still being side-stepped by tourists who think he might be a beggar, a thief, who think he might be trouble.

She moves away from the window slightly and picks up the rope. She wound it around her arm, around her elbow, over her knuckles. Then she moved it up to her throat and held it there for a moment. She squeezed ever so slightly, just enough to feel her breath struggle and a light dizziness settle in the top of her head. She took the rope away from her throat and held it in her hand again. A strange heaviness filled up her middle, moved around her insides and then settled.

She thought she recognised the feeling, but couldn't make sense of it being with her now. It was pulled from somewhere in her that she wasn't aware of. It was weighed with the words, *my fault.*

When she looked out into the road again he'd gone. She strained her neck and tried to see up the road, tried to catch a glimpse of his legs as he walked round the bend in the narrow street, but he'd gone. She scanned the people in the street for his hair, his back, his face, but she didn't see him.

*

Stress is a funny thing. That's what she'd said. That's what she told him. A funny thing. It doesn't have a form. You can't see it. You can't pass a hand over it and feel it bump under your touch. You can't tell if it's there at all. In some ways it only exists to the person who is experiencing it. Them, and whoever has to live with them.

She'd kept it as vague as she could and Matthew had asked for no further details. He was afraid of the response he might get if he did. Like a rush of water. A broken pipe. There would be no way to get away from it once it had started.

So it was stress. It was a stress thing. They had decided as much in unspoken signs and feelings. But Matthew could feel the end. He could sense it like he could sense the end of the rope about to pass through his hand. And what would they say then? How would they name it once they had run out of cover-ups?

He sat down in the street, staring into the thin road. He was aware of people all around him, stepping over his legs, looking at him and tutting. He had crossed a line up there in the flat and he had no idea what was next. But it would be bad, he knew that. It would be a thing that any rational person would stay away from as long as possible.

He couldn't go back into the flat now. God knows how he could face her after all that. Besides, he needed a little time to himself. To think. To get his story straight. He got up from his sitting position by the road. One or two people passed him, making a show of moving out of his way. He took a deep breath and headed for the nearest pub, the Pilot Boat Inn.

*

Melanie had her hair dyed the colour of cherries. It was loosely plaited at either side of her head, the twisted braids tapering down to below her collarbone. It made her look sweet with her hair like this, Anthony thought. Like Hiawatha or an Austrian milking maid. She wore a black T-shirt with an explosion of colour in the middle of it, and a black zip-up coat which hung lazily on her shoulders as she walked beside him. This was before she moved away and stopped talking to him, before his dad died and he fell apart; but then, as both Melanie and Anthony know very well, Anthony was slowly falling apart in the months before Peter died.

They walked together through the quiet streets in Lyme Regis, where they had both lived all their lives.

"If you could go anywhere, where would you go?" she asked him.

Anthony swung her small hand as they walked, feeling her soft fingers clasping his. He shrugged. "Dunno," he said. "Anywhere would be better than here. Where would you go?"

"Canada," she said. "Or somewhere else cold. Somewhere really cold. Somewhere no one else goes."

He grinned at her. He loved the things she said, loved the way she said them, loved everything that was going on in that complicated mind of hers.

"Let's go somewhere else then," he said.

Melanie stopped walking and leaned her body from him as if she was sizing him up. "When?" she asked.

Anthony swung her hand playfully again. "Right now," he said. "I'll get dad's car and we'll drive out and go somewhere else."

She smiled. "That's not what I meant."

"I know," he said. "But it's a start."

They walked up the hill, crossed the road at the top, passed the bus stop and walked on until they could just see the *Welcome to Devon* sign sloping down the opposite hill. They walked up the path to Anthony's house.

It was only when Melanie saw the roof emerge from

behind the trees and then the brick of the building, that she stopped.

"What's up?"

Melanie looked at Anthony, her body tense. "Maybe this isn't a good idea," she said.

"Huh?"

"I mean, me going to your house, maybe... with your dad..."

"Don't be silly," Anthony said. "It'll be fine, anyway, my dad won't be in."

"Are you sure?"

"Yeah," he shrugged. "Though it's not as if you're going to be able to avoid him for ever. He is my dad."

She started to walk forward with Anthony again now, reassured that his dad wouldn't be in.

They reached the front door and Anthony had pushed it open, and they'd stepped inside, before Melanie saw that Peter was there after all.

Inside the house Anthony's dad shoved his hand into his trouser pocket, brought out his car keys and tossed them over to Anthony. Anthony caught them, said, "Cheers Dad," and turned to go, Melanie already halfway out of the door as fast as she could.

Melanie had been going out with him for two years now, and she had always been comfortable in his parents' house, at ease. But everything had changed at work on Friday afternoon, the day before. And she could now feel the creeping sense of how that would soon change everything else. Everything.

They left the house, the orange glow from the dim sidelights in the living room behind them. They walked on the gravel driveway, each footstep crunching the scattered fragments of rock under their feet. They could see the grooves the tyres of the car had made in the gravel when Peter had brought the car up here and parked it earlier on that evening. They walked to either side of the car. Anthony held up the keys and unlocked the car, and they both slid inside.

They drove to Beer, a village smaller and quieter than

Lyme. Anthony made a joke about how much beer he would drink in Beer. And Melanie said, when she'd mentioned wanting to go somewhere else, she meant somewhere more exciting than where they lived, not somewhere deader.

They parked the car and walked down to the pebble beach. The first hopeful days of summer had warmed the water a little and the days were growing longer and longer. Two women and four kids stood and played by the water's edge. The eldest boy and the eldest girl, about 14 years old, teased each other in the sea. She sat on a rock like a siren and he flicked salt water at her. The game couldn't be stopped. Hormones and curiosity fought inside the both of them, until the boy went too far and flung seaweed, cold and ruined, onto the girl's bare shoulder, and she left the rock and the shore, confused by his need to humiliate her. Melanie and Anthony watched, then turned and smiled at each other like an old knowing couple: *Remember when we were that age? Remember when we were innocent?*

They walked for a while, but it was really no different to their own pebble beach, so they walked back, away from the sea, and they found a pub.

It wasn't exactly an argument. They were standing up, leaning against a pillar in the pub, and Melanie was talking about work. Anthony felt an internal groan make its way across his chest and begin to rise. He should have changed the subject there and then. He should never have spoken at all. But it was her fault. She would just keep going on about it.

"Do you think it will bother him?" she asked.

Anthony could feel the blood rising, and at the same time something else sinking inside him.

“”Of course it will bother him," he said. "What do you expect?"

Melanie was biting her lip. She drained her glass and held it out to him. "But that isn't my fault, is it? I can't hold back just because he won't like it."

Anthony swiped the empty glass from Melanie's hand and downed what was left in his own glass, then he turned away from her and went to the bar to have their glasses refilled. He was annoyed with her for bringing all this up tonight. Anthony had taken her out for a celebration drink last night, even though he already had a sense that he wasn't sure whether he should be celebrating. He thought they were supposed to be getting away from everything tonight.

When he returned to their table, he put her drink down in front of Melanie and sat his own in his cupped hands.

"How much have you had to drink?" she asked.

"Not much, I'm fine."

"You can't drive if you've had too much, we'll need to get a taxi and..."

"I said I'm fine, you know alcohol doesn't affect me, you know I don't get drunk easy."

"Yeah, but..."

"Stop going on, Mel, you're always going on about *something*."

Melanie stopped speaking for a minute and stared at him. He was angry. No matter how much he tried to tell her the situation she was in at work was fine with him, it clearly wasn't. He was angry about it.

"You don't seriously think I should turn the promotion down, do you?" she asked. "Just because he didn't get the job and I did."

Anthony took another gulp of his pint. "Doesn't matter what I think, does it?" he said.

Well, did it?

No, she would have to say, when it came down to it, it didn't matter what Anthony thought about this. And it didn't matter if his dad hated her for being his boss now and their easy comfortable relationship while Melanie glided through their house every Sunday morning and spent almost every evening of the week sitting on their sofa, suddenly became strained because she got the promotion and Peter didn't and she, twenty-seven years younger than him, and exactly half his age, was now his boss.

They didn't speak so much after that in the pub. Anthony was quiet and Melanie tried to talk about the problem with the leaky windows in the flat and how the downstairs was being used as a holiday flat to rent now, but the conversation was already lost.

She noticed him drinking, of course she did. What could she say? That she'd been too annoyed with him for his attitude about her job to try and stop him? That she hadn't cared? That she'd lost the will to try and tell him what to do?

When they got outside they both just slid into the car as if there was no problem at all. They didn't speak now. Melanie can't remember when their anger and frustration with each other over her promotion had halted all words that night, but it had, and they sat silently as Anthony fumbled with the engine and turned the car sharply out of the car park.

*

He walked up by The Angel, the pub that was supposedly haunted. The thought made him tighten inside. He walked up past the car park. Up, and then to the right, through the streets until he came to the road that Melanie was living in while she was here. He stopped and stood in the dark street. Thought for the first time tonight what he would say to her. She wasn't expecting him to turn up here. Anthony thought that must be a good thing. It was just the way she had gone about things that bothered him. Moving away. Coming back. Never telling him. Never contacting him or saying a word about any of it. Never keeping in touch. Why didn't she just find him, call him, go to the house? But, he supposed, she would hardly want to do that. She would hardly be welcomed by anyone else at his house.

He walked slowly towards the front door. He unfolded the paper again and checked the house number. She would be shocked to see him here at this time of night. She would know that he had come to her via Kate. She would know that Kate had come clean and told him everything. But that didn't matter. Kate was nothing to the two of them.

He breathed in the cold, sharp air, felt it fill his nose, throat, and then his lungs. He let it out again, and with it felt his nerves burst open and his heart begin to beat faster. He walked up to the door and knocked.

*

She was scared, but, stupidly she would think later, the argument was still taut between them, still coiled, and it held everything inside of her while he drove down the roads, too fast, too unaware of everything else, it seemed to her. She'd been drinking too, and maybe that's what saved her from an overflowing of fear. But then, too little fear also meant that she said nothing to Anthony as he cut corners in half, almost mounted curbs and swerved in the road over the central lines.

She held the sides of the seat by her legs and felt her body tense, but she never really thought anything would happen. She never actually believed that he would lose control.

*

He stands on the step. The light from inside the house pours over him as she opens the door.

"Anthony!" She stands there for a minute, eyes wide in the fading light. "What happened to you?"

"I was in a fight, it's nothing."

"Doesn't look like nothing!"

"Yeah, well, it doesn't matter." He takes a breath. "Anyway..." He stares at her.

She leans her head and her body on one side in a gesture of impatience, then opens the door wider and stands back for him to enter.

"*She* told you where I was, didn't she!" Melanie says.

"You've cut your hair," he says, stepping past her into the house.

"People keep saying that. As if I didn't know it already."

Anthony steps inside the house and walks past her as she closes the door. "What people?" he asks.

"Your mum for one."

He lets her pass him in the hallway and then he follows her. "You've seen my mum?"

"Didn't she tell you?"

*

They were sitting together in the living room now. A small spindly Christmas tree glistened in the corner, wilting, leaning towards the flat screen TV. The rough brown sofa they sat on had a purple throw hanging halfway on, halfway off its arm. The floor was simple bare floorboards, not even polished. The air smelled of something sweet, and stale at the same time.

"Why didn't *you* tell me you were in town?" he said. "Did you think I wouldn't talk to you?"

Melanie made a slight shrug forward with her shoulders. "Of course," she said. "It hardly ended well, did it? I thought you might still be angry with me."

Anthony could feel a frown ruffle his head. "I was never angry with you," he said. "It wasn't your fault. It was all my fault, the way I acted, everything, the night we went to Beer, it was all my fault, there's no wonder you left."

"But about your dad…" Melanie said. "About me getting the job and everything, I thought you'd be angry with me about all that. And I had to leave after all that, I had to get away."

"Is that why you left then? Just because of that? Not because of what I did? So why didn't you even tell me where you were going? You never told anyone, you just went."

Melanie rubbed her palms together between her knees as if she was cold, but it was only nerves. She nodded. "It seemed like the best thing."

*

He was driving too fast. She knew that. The road curved around the edge of the land like forced breaths, in and out with an even rhythm. But the bends were getting the better of him. When the car went off the road Melanie had no sense of what was going on. One minute everything was sound, the next nothing added up. Melanie felt like her head was pressed against the roof of the car, and then she was in free fall, her whole body distorted. She could see sky and ground tumbling and spinning, and she realised the car was rolling down the hill. It stopped after a few moments. She breathed. Made sure she still could. Then she checked which way up she was. The car was righted. They were still for a moment and then, neither of them speaking, Anthony and Melanie both undid their seat belts and opened their car doors. They stood. Then they began walking away from the car, back up to the road.

Anthony stood in one place and flagged down the next car that came. He stood by the open window and asked the driver to give them a lift. Melanie had already walked away from him a few metres down the road. He ran to catch her up once he'd explained to the driver of the car what had happened. "Just lost control," he said to the man in the car. And the man looked at him. He could see in that one moment the whole of the evening. The drinking. An argument. Driving fast and the car turning over down the hill because Anthony had lost control.

Anthony ran down the road and secured Melanie in his arms. She didn't react at all. Just stood there while he held onto her as if she would drift away from him if he let go. Behind them, sitting in the driver's seat of the waiting car, the man called the police. Melanie could see his face while he spoke down the phone line, the way his eyes watched her and Anthony as if they might run at any minute.

Melanie struggled slightly in Anthony's grasp. "We have to go back," she said. "To the car."

He turned to follow her eyes back up the road. The man was getting out of the car and opening the boot as Anthony and Melanie walked back up the road. The man turned to them as they approached, a curl of rope in his hands. "Don't suppose it's much use really," he said. He spoke as if Anthony and Melanie weren't really there. "Don't really know why I still keep it in here." Then he turned to Melanie. He wouldn't look at Anthony yet. "Tow rope," he said. "We could probably pull your car back onto the road..." then he let the rope fall. "Naw, best not," he went on. "I reckon police would have something to say, I bet they won't want it touched."

She remembers being at the house after. They'd waited on the road back to Lyme with the flagged-down car. The driver telling them he'd had to call the police. "You're drunk." And then Anthony's head falling into his own hands. What seemed like hours after, but wasn't, a policeman making an arrest in his mind before Anthony was even out of the car. There was no getting away from this.

She got a lift back to the house after, in a police car. She knew it wasn't really his fault, knew these things are slipped in under people's skins without them even realising it sometimes, but she could feel the way the policeman looked at her, could almost read his thoughts and the ease with which he connected together in his brain the way she appeared, her dyed hair, the clothes she wore, the way Anthony looked, with what he had done. He would probably say as much to someone back at the station later, *Did you see them? No wonder, is there?*

She stood in front of Peter back at the house and she felt his despair over his son. "He could have killed someone," he said. "He could have killed himself… stupid… stupid."

She watched and became aware of herself shrivelling.

"…Or you!" Peter said, his hand flying out in front of him, a sharp gesture in Melanie's direction. But she was an afterthought, she knew that. Peter didn't care. He would have preferred almost anyone to be saved from the potential disaster and car crash over Melanie. She would be one less problem to him if she was dead. One less thing to worry his muddled head if she was gone.

She stood there for a second, waiting for him to ask her if she was OK, could he get her anything, did she need to sit down, but he didn't. He stared at the carpet then he looked up sharply at her, the white hair only a passing thought on his head, his blue eyes cold like spring wind. "My car!" he said. "What about my car?" Then other thoughts chased the first shock and began to settle in his head. "The insurance. The bloody insurance."

Melanie stared at him, a sudden feeling of exhaustion dragging inside her. "What?"

"The bloody insurance won't pay, not if he was over the limit. Oh, that's all I bloody need. As if we aren't in enough of a mess as it is."

*

She went through to the kitchen. Anthony trailed behind her, afraid to let her out of his sight in case she disappeared again. She took two brown pottery mugs down from a cupboard and dropped a teabag into one of them. The lino on the small kitchen floor was peeling up at the corners of the room. Anthony could see the black grime where the floor underneath was exposed. Melanie never seemed to notice things like that. In the flat she used to live in the windows were constantly running with condensation and spare rainwater, but Melanie never paid it any attention, leaving the pools to subside and dry on their own, causing dirty stains and brown puddle marks on the wooden sills.

He looked around the cold kitchen while Melanie squeezed out the teabag and then dropped it into the second mug.

"Whose house is this anyway?"

She didn't look up. "Friends," she said. "Someone I used to work with, said I could have my mail delivered here and stuff, like a forwarding address, and then, when I wanted to come back for a bit..." she shrugged, "I had a place to stay."

Anthony was picking apart each movement she made while she spoke, each change in her expression. "A man?" he asked. "Is it a man?"

She shook her head and laughed a little. "For God's sake, Anthony, is that all you can think of?"

He retracted for a moment. Tried to fathom what was going on inside a woman. Why wouldn't he have thought that?

"Why did you come back, Mel?" he asked. "What's so important you'd come all this way for? Is it because of Dad?"

She stirred the tea slowly and looked at him.

"Yes, and other things. Everything really. I went up to the house. I saw your mum. I wanted to... apologise."

"Apologise? You mean about Dad? About the promotion? Is that what this is all about?"

"It is about your dad," she said. "About what he did. I just can't… I can't not talk about it anymore. I need to tell you, it was my fault."

*

Melanie was sick of having no money. She'd made a decision and she'd felt it take hold of her insides and set everything straight in her head. It was time to grow up. Time to be in control. Time to make her life work. She'd put herself forward and applied for promotion. No way she would get it, she kept telling herself. No way they would choose her over Peter. Peter who had been with the company for thirty years and knew every millimetre of the rope factory inside out. Peter who had miles of experience stretching out behind the person he was today. Peter who was dependable. Older. Wiser. A man.

But going through the motions would be a good thing anyway, Melanie decided. The interview and the process would help her. She could take a lot away from that alone. So she made the decision. She didn't tell Anthony at first. After all, it was his dad she was going up against. No way she would beat him to the post though.

When she did tell Anthony his face had frozen and he'd sucked all his usual softness back inside himself somewhere and he'd stared at her.

"You are kidding?" he said.

She'd shaken her head mutely and watched his face, then she said, "I won't get it. I don't stand a chance. Peter will get it, we all know that, everybody says so."

Her words were a subtle double bluff. Anthony could see that. The very fact that she spoke them meant that she held a secret file inside her heart that whispered to her. She knew she stood every chance of getting that job. Hoped she would land it and steal it out from under Peter's nose. She knew she was better than Peter at what she did. More dynamic. Faster. More willing. Flexible. Younger. A woman.

"Then why apply?" Anthony said.

It slapped her in the face. Why apply? Was that the kind of thing he should be saying to her? Why bother? If she knew she wouldn't get it, why even bother applying?

She stumbled. "Because... because I have to seem interested, or they won't consider me in the future, they'll say 'Why didn't you apply for the last promotion?' They'll be expecting me to apply, even though they probably already know who'll get it. They've probably already decided. You know these things are a formality, but I still have to apply or they'll never take me seriously."

Anthony eyed her, his head tilted slightly away from her. She could see that he didn't believe her. Wondered if she even believed herself.

"Don't know why you want the stupid job anyway," he said.

The day it was announced that Melanie had bagged it, had cleaned up and had taken the promotion and all that came with it, she thought she saw something fade out of Peter. It was his last chance, she could see that. There would be no other. He was getting too old now and he wouldn't be considered for any future positions. Would be laughed out of the office. She watched him as he hesitantly clapped along with everyone else, his eyes twitching to either side of him, sure everyone was really looking at him and not at Melanie, sure they were all whispering about him. Poor old Peter. Didn't get it. Was overtaken by a mere girl.

Melanie stood at the front of the office and smiled as she was congratulated, her hand shaken, her arm touched affectionately by those who would now become her staff, and she saw Peter move forward towards her. He was still clapping along with everyone else. Someone leaned in and said, "Well done Melanie, we knew you'd do it."

She was still watching Peter, but she glanced at the person standing nearest to her for a moment. Did they? Did they really know that she would get it? Is that what they'd all been saying in the canteen and outside while they smoked? All those things she'd convinced herself that everyone said about Peter.

She must have looked a little confused as Peter approached her, his heavily freckled hands still moving in a slow clap, his blue eyes showing just the slightest hint of pain, his smile a defeat. "Well done," he said. "The best man won."

Melanie let go of her frown and tried to smile. "No hard feelings?" she asked.

And Peter turned and walked away.

*

"You were right," Melanie said. "I should never have gone for that stupid job. I should have just let him have it. He deserved it, and he would have retired soon anyway and then I could have gone for promotion. I should have waited. Maybe Peter would still be here."

Anthony was staring at her. Her short dark hair made her look older, and he didn't think living abroad was doing her any favours. The sun was drying her skin and she looked tired. Anthony imagined her staying up late, partying too much, drinking wine at lunch time and napping in the afternoon.

"Is that what you thought?" he asked. "That it was your fault? Because you got the job?"

"He never *really* liked me," Melanie said. "And once I was his boss he hated me. But it was more than that. I was younger than him and a woman. A man of your dad's age just couldn't accept it. He'd worked there most of his life. He couldn't start taking orders from me."

Anthony was shaking his head. "That's what you thought? That's why you left Lyme altogether?"

"It made things between you and me too difficult..."

"But you didn't need to leave the country!"

"I only left when it happened. It was only when he did what he did."

"You mean you only moved to Portugal *after* he died... so, that means earlier this month?"

"It was all my fault, Anthony. How could you ever forgive me for that?"

"It wasn't your fault, of course it wasn't," Anthony instinctively started to say the right thing, even though they both knew full well that things had changed for his dad once he'd missed out on the promotion. Still, that didn't make it her fault. Anthony knew he was the only one to blame. And if Melanie's promotion had contributed to Peter's suicide in some small way – the promotion that it turned out she hadn't really wanted so badly after all – even that could be traced back to him: it was he who had told Melanie about the job going at the rope factory in the first place. So everything was his fault, even more so.

"You had nothing to do with what he did," he continued.

"But I did!"

"You didn't. He made his own choice, how can that have been your fault?"

"Because of what I said, on that day, before he did it. Because maybe I was the last person he spoke to and the only possible explanation is that he did it because of what I said!"

He still couldn't say it. The words were bottled. Secured insidc him. They tasted of sickness, of death. *It wasn't your fault. It was me. It was all me.*

He looked to the floor in the little kitchen. Half of the strip lighting on the ceiling was gone, snuffed out, and the dank lino beneath his feet looked more dingy in the half light. He still held his hand around the hot mug on the side of the sink. In front of him Melanie waited for a response. What was he supposed to say? Should he tell her he forgave her? That it was all in the past, didn't matter now. Should he beg her to come back? Is that what she wanted?

He traced a stray drop of liquid around the rim of the mug with his finger. Didn't look up. "So, that's it. That's why you're here...?" he said.

"Yes, of course that's why I'm here. I couldn't stop thinking about it. I thought it if I left the country, went away...

but it didn't work, I just felt terrible."

He looked at her now. Could see the pain in her face, her eyes searching him for something. Forgiveness? He couldn't stand it. She had nothing to feel that way about. "Don't be silly, Mel," he said quietly. "You have nothing to feel bad about."

"Of course I do, Anthony, I took away his hope, you know that, you said yourself..."

He shook his head. "No, you didn't. Don't say that. You're..." He moved forward and went to touch her arm, but she moved backwards. The word "perfect" stayed in his throat.

"I needed to... set things straight before I can move on," she said. "I needed to talk to you and tell you and... say I'm sorry, that's why I came back so soon, but then when I got here... the idea of it all seemed so easy while I was in Portugal. I'd come back, see you, your mum maybe, we'd talk. But then as soon as I got here it all seemed so different, and when it came to it I thought, you know, I'd be the last person you'd want to see."

He could hear in her words that she was asking him to contradict her. And it was true. How could she ever be the last person he would want to see? But he didn't say it.

So she came back because she felt guilty, because she believed it was her fault. She came all this way in the hope that it would somehow make her feel better. She didn't come back to see him at all.

He couldn't say another word. Nothing was working properly. His speech stayed in his throat and he couldn't look at her. He touched the mug again. It was too hot. He could feel the burn through the cup. She wanted to move on. He turned quickly and left the house, the front door banging behind him.

*

She hears his feet, the weight of his body making them land heavy on each stair. She imagines his hand steadying him against the wall as he takes the steep stairs two at a time. She hears the door open and bang slightly onto the wall behind it. Then he has closed it again and he is inside. She won't say anything. And neither will he.

She touches the rope, its three strands winding round one another from end to end.

Then Matthew is in the room. He falls onto the sofa, picks up the remote and aims it at the TV. He doesn't speak. He doesn't look at her.

"You OK?" she asks.

Fear shoots through her middle, splitting her like a crack in wet wood. She'd never seen Matthew like that before. She felt herself at an edge of something. He knew she'd been lying, that was bad enough. What would he be like if he knew all of it?

He nods. "Er, yeah," he says. "Sorry." Then he moves his body on the sofa and looks at her, his brown eyes, his mouth. She watches the way his face works. There's a hardness still beneath his skin. He doesn't look like he's sorry. "Hope I didn't hurt you, it's just…"

She makes herself smile. "You didn't. Let's not talk about it."

She actually smiles. He hadn't hurt her. And she was relieved they were talking, he said he was sorry. At least he said it. He was sorry. *It's just…*

"Are you gonna be ready to go back to work after Christmas, or what?"

She didn't answer for a moment. She thought through the burn in her throat and chest at the mention of work.

"Don't know," she said.

"You have to go back sometime."

"I know, but… I'm not ready."

"Maybe you'll never feel ready, but you have to go back."

"The doctor signed me off," she said.

"The longer you leave it the harder it will be, and… come on…"

Kate felt a tickle of anger mix with the dread. "Come on what?"

"There's nothing wrong with you."

Kate stood there behind the sofa. His words, the way he said it, there's nothing wrong with you, made her feel he didn't care at all. He couldn't see what was wrong with her. It didn't have a colour, a shape, a smell or even a name, at least not that she knew of. The doctor had known. He fitted it into a box on his computer screen and he'd signed papers that said she should stay home and take pills. He told her she had suffered, and she thought about Peter again, thought about what Anthony had said, *He suffered for years*, though with what she didn't know. Kate's doctor had known. He'd made it all seem so normal and everyday. She had suffered a mental intrusion, he said. As if some solid, organic entity had rammed its way into her brain and would keep on doing so until the pills were all swallowed and thick in her bloodstream. A mental intrusion.

"I told you, it's stress. I can't go back yet, I'm not ready."

She saw Matthew turn to the TV again, shimmy his shoulders as he lay back down on the sofa. He didn't believe her. Why should he? She was lying.

*

He'd never had an affair. He told himself that's what separated him from other men. Other men who couldn't keep it in their pants and had no self-control. He'd never done anything. Never acted on it. And anyway, he reasoned, it was unnatural to expect to be with the same person all these years and never meet anyone else, never fancy anyone else. It was what you did about it that mattered. And Peter had never done anything.

She still found out though. It was typical. There were hundreds of men out their sleeping around behind their wives' backs and never getting caught. Peter didn't do that. But Susie still found out.

The first time it happened she was hurt. He'd been seen in The Volunteer, having a drink with a woman. Some well-meaning busybody had asked Susie who her husband was out having drinks with, and she'd been hurt. She asked him and he told her the truth. He realised after that that was a mistake.

Anthony was small at the time. His older brothers were loud and difficult, and he just needed... escape, he told her. Nothing had happened, it was just a drink. But Susie didn't see it like that.

Years later he'd met someone while walking his dog through the undercliff. They'd chatted at first, the way you do when out with dogs, the way dogs bring people together like that. Then they'd started meeting at the same time. Every day. But nothing happened. They'd flirted... with the idea more than anything, but nothing actually happened.

When Susie found out and he'd told her that very thing, she'd screamed at him. "You think that makes it OK?"

He supposed he had for a while. He supposed he'd thought it was OK. He'd made excuses for himself and he rationalised it away. It was nothing. It didn't mean anything. They were just friends.

But this time was different.

This time it felt urgent. Like he was running out of time. Like she could be the antidote. Like he needed her in some way. Like, with his debts and Melanie getting the promotion instead of him and everything that was shit about his life, Kate could be the only thing that would give him the kind of outlet he needed.

*

Peter had come to her with a smile high in his face. Kate had been working at the rope factory for about a month when she noticed the funny way he was looking at her. She'd heard all the gossip soon enough after starting the job. The head of her department was still quite new, and trying to push her weight around a bit. Kate remembered what her new friend had told her in the canteen. "But Peter should have got that job, everyone said so, everyone thought he'd get it, but *she* took it instead. Don't think Peter's ever got over it."

Kate looked slowly at Peter. Did that have something to do with the funny way he was staring at her? Did he despise her, blame her in some way for coming in and filling a gap made by this woman who had taken his promotion away from him? It didn't make any sense. Wasn't rational. But at least it explained the way he was looking at her.

One day she was walking down the stairs after her break and Peter was coming up the other way. They were about to cross on the stairway, something that always pressed a silent alarm button inside of Kate, her dead grandmother's warning entering the front of her mind. *Never cross on the stairs.* Kate had not asked why, what terrible thing would happen if she did this. And then not so long ago she read a paperback where a man and a woman do cross on the stairs and they swapped souls there and then. She glanced at Peter as he rounded the stairway towards her and she thought about what it would be like to swap souls with this man. He had a good position here in the company. Much higher up than Kate. So the money would be better if she found herself trapped inside his body. But he was a man and Kate didn't know if she could handle that. Worst of all, he was an old man, almost ready for retirement surely. She thought that over. That wouldn't be such a bad thing, apart from the fact that she would have missed out huge chunks of her life.

Kate must have been smiling while she thought about all this. It must have shown on her face in some way because Peter stopped when he was almost level with her. She looked down at him and he stared back. He stood there and stared long enough for Kate to say, "What?"

He just shook his head, a tinge of embarrassment showing around his ears, and he walked on up the stairs.

Another time she was sitting at her desk when he walked right up and put his hands face down in front of her on the clear wooden surface. And he stood there and stared at her like the moment was significant. Like he was about to say something. Like it was really important. But he didn't say anything. He just stood there, his body slightly hunched forward, his eyes searching her, though she didn't know what for. Kate looked at him. Waited for a moment. Then she felt a rush of impatience. She was busy. Didn't have time for this. If she'd done something wrong he should just come out with it. If he needed something from her he should just say it. But he just looked at her. Like a boy at school intimidated by a girl. Only he wasn't a boy, was he? And as he stood there she began to feel uncomfortable.

"Yes?" she said, a tiny snap in her voice, a flair of annoyance in her face.

Peter stood up straight again. "No, nothing," he said. "I was just…" and he turned and walked away again.

Kate spent weeks peering at him from the corner of her vision, thinking he had a problem with her. He didn't like her. He had something he wanted to say, some issue with her work, but for some reason couldn't find the words or the right time to bring it up. So he kept coming up to her or looking at her in that way he did and never actually said much of anything at all.

She began thinking more carefully about what she was doing. She didn't want to lose this job. Kate and Matthew didn't have much spare money after they'd paid the bills and bought food so dropping a wage would be disastrous.

Then after work one evening, in the pub for a colleague's leaving drinks, Kate saw a clear light shine.

In the pub Peter sat along the table from Kate, on the same side with two other people in between them. Still, she could feel him look at her.

"But you don't want to work in that factory forever though do you?" someone said.

"I don't really," Kate said. "But what else could *I* do?"

"You could do anything," Peter said. He threw the words out over the table. "Anything you want."

It was a new thought. She could do anything. She was really that free.

Then later at the bar she fumbled in her purse to buy drinks and Peter stood beside her. Kind of stout. White hair cropped so short on top of his head where there was hardly any left. So short it stood on end. Too much of it still at the back of his head where he tried to hold onto some link to his younger years, where it lay and rippled about his neck like slow waves on a calm sea. It needed cutting shorter and she wanted to tell him so.

He turned to her and smiled, high in his face, not revealing his teeth. The kind of smile that shows you aren't sure of the reaction you'll get. He'd had a few drinks. He'd drunk pints of Guinness the colour of a black cat's fur. He was ordering another and he said, "I'll get them. What would you like?"

What would she like? There. In that moment. What would she most like? The way he said it made her think he would give her anything. No matter what she came up with, no matter what extravagances she conjured up from her mind and her throat, he would give them to her.

She looked at his eyes, cornflower blue, and she didn't see anything else except his soul. The one she might easily have swapped with him on the stairs that time. She wondered how it would feel inside of her. She wondered how deep it would go, what it was like, what he was really like.

She gave him the order from the table, including white wine for herself. She waited with him while the drinks were served. Watched his hands, browned by years of sun, his arms the same but with a covering of white hairs so gentle they appeared like a whisper on his skin.

He pushed the wine glass towards her and said, "There you go."

This time he couldn't look at her. It was all too much. It was out. It was obvious. She knew now why he had spent so many open moments at work just looking at her without any words between them. Why he had stopped and stared. Why he had turned up at her desk as if he was about to say something and then felt the words stop in his chest, and he'd walked away again without speaking a single one. And now it was out things would never be the same. She touched the stem of the glass where his fingers still waited, pushing it towards her on the bar. She saw his wedding ring, thin like a shepherd moon. She brushed her fingertips against his as she took the glass from him. And there was no going back.

After that, at work, Kate wasn't sure how to act around him. Peter didn't seem to have the same problem. If she looked up from her desk and located his face in the room it was always looking back at her. He lingered in the doorway at lunch time. Followed her around. Opened doors. She could see it in his face how much he cared. How he thought something had started. How he was waiting for it to continue. He pushed forward with his feelings and he forced it all towards her. She couldn't stop it.

"You want a lift home after work?" he asked one day, with his head leant back slightly as if he was waiting for a blow to hit the underside of his chin.

She shrugged. "Sure."

And it seemed for a moment like such a simple thing. They both lived in the same village. Why had neither of them never thought of it before? In that one moment it seemed so simple, innocent, easy. In that one isolated moment it could be a throwaway action. It was only a lift. But barely a few minutes after she'd accepted his offer the doubt played and moved in her brain. She looked around her across the open plan office. No-one would have been able to overhear, but it was bound to be noticed when they left together. She could already feel the looks from her colleagues, could almost hear the whispers before they began. It was only a lift. But it was so much more than that.

*

She'd got up in the morning early and started to busy herself around the flat. She had a feeling that Matthew was awake, but was avoiding opening his eyes, avoiding speaking to her or even looking at her. She could see the side of his face and his dark mass of hair on the pillow, duvet pulled up around his neck and she watched him for a moment, the swell and fall of his breathing. It was hard to imagine how they would bring an end to him and her. The details of it. But maybe she'd have to think about it soon.

She began loading the washing into the machine. As she stood up and switched it on she could hear Matthew move in the bedroom, his bulky form heavy as he stood up. She couldn't imagine being here and not hearing that, not having Matthew there, not seeing him. Or worse, maybe she'd have to move back in at her mum's. That was almost unthinkable. But what he'd done, tying her up. That was unthinkable too. Just a quick "sorry" wasn't enough. Especially, *Sorry, it's just...*

He walked slowly through from the bedroom, sleep still

in his face, hair messy. He leaned on the worktop and looked at her. She glanced back. She couldn't read him, but she could feel that there was something he wanted to say, needed to ask, there was something.

"Are you OK?" he asked. "I mean, really?"

"What?"

"It's just... you know I care about you, you know I love you."

Kate stopped what she was doing and stood up straight. "I'm fine," she said. "Why are you asking me now?"

Matthew shrugged. He touched a cup on the drainer, the handle smooth and curved in like the small of Kate's back. "Just wondered," he said. "You just seem so... I know, about *the thing,* but…You know you can tell me, tell me anything."

He looked at her and he saw her release a small laugh, as if the idea that she would tell him anything was so stupid.

He turned and stared at the cup on the drainer for a moment. He was still pressing his fingers up and down the handle, feeling the curve between his thumb and forefinger.

"I'm sorry about all that business with the rope, you know, me bringing it home and... I got it wrong, but..." He moved the words around on his tongue, began to sort them and choose which to say, which to keep. "Anyway, I'm sorry."

"Is that it? Sorry? Is that the best you can do?"

Matthew stared at her. "What else do you want?"

"I want you to talk to me. I mean really talk to me. I want you to tell me what the hell you were thinking. How could you do a thing like that? How could you do that to me? And then to just carry on as if nothing's happened."

"But you said you didn't want to talk about it. You said, let's not talk about it."

"I meant I didn't want to talk about it right then, at that moment, not I didn't want to talk about it ever!"

"Well how was I supposed to know that?"

He could see her breathing through her nose, anger still in her at what he'd done. But he'd said he was sorry. What else could he do?

"Maybe that's the problem, Matt."

"What?"

"You should know. You should just know."

He reached forward and tried to take her hand. "I just want us to go back to how we were before. I just want things to be like they used to be."

"But things aren't how they were before, are they?"

"No," he said. "But it isn't just me, Kate, you can't lay all the blame for that on me."

There was a feeling then, light in the air between them, that the truth was out. Just for a moment. Just for a second it swam in the space where they looked at each other. He didn't know. He didn't know anything. He had no idea what was going on. And she acknowledged it. They looked at each other.

"That funeral you went to," he said. He angled his head in towards the cup, the feel of it on his skin keeping him connected to normality. She didn't show any sign that she'd heard him, but he carried on. "How was it?"

She didn't look at him now, but slowed down her hands for a minute as she laid out the knives and forks on the table.

"It was a funeral," she said. "It was sad. How else would a funeral be?"

"And just remind me again," Matthew said. "Who was it that died?"

"Peter. I told you."

Matthew moved away from the drainer a little, dipping his head and trying to catch her eyes. "And why was Peter important to you?" he asked. He let go of the cup and moved towards her. He pushed her hair away from her face and almost took her chin and forced her to look at him, but she shook him off.

"Kate, come on," he said. "I'm trying here. I'm really trying. I want us to put all this behind us, get back to how we used to be."

"And how do we do that?"

"By working through it, together."

She let out another sarcastic laugh. "God, Matt, you sound like a self-help book or something."

"Well, do you want to?" he asked. "If we both want to make this work we can do it, I know we can, we can get through anything. So, do you want to?"

She paused and stared at him for a second, then she made a move to leave the kitchen. "I don't know, Matt," she said. "I really don't know."

She stands in the living room and looks out onto the narrow street. The windows are lined with condensation and the towels she pushes into the corners of the sill are always damp. Outside, different lives go on. She thinks about how different life could be. What it might be like to be someone else, even somewhere else.

Up above the village, where the shops and restaurants end and large quiet houses huddle, away from the sea and welcoming drivers who cross the border, is the *Welcome to Devon* sign. A whole new county. Kate had seen that sign many times. As a child she hadn't really understood what it meant. As an adult she'd felt the lure of change and new beginnings it offered.

She stands in the living room now, tired of this flat and the tension within it, tired of living in this village with the awkwardness of all that has happened.

She wonders what it would be like to live on the other side. She wonders if she could leave everything she has here and start again, over that invisible line, in Devon, away from the weight of sadness and the feeling that she will never escape who she is here. Become someone else.

*

Peter was dead. Peter was a guy whose funeral she'd been to. He was dead. But Matthew knew that. She said this whole thing, all this trouble, all this mess, was about Peter. But Peter had gone.

So did she really have such strong feelings for him? She said she hadn't had an affair with him, but Matthew had seen what he had seen: his eyes hadn't been deceiving him. So was she telling him the truth or not?

He folded his confusion deep down in his body, felt it weigh heavy as he pushed it down further. There had to be another reason, another explanation, something he couldn't see yet. Had to be. But wherever he turned he found the same outcome. Her nerves were a mess. She was hiding stuff from him. Not telling him things. She wouldn't have sex with him. Wouldn't even get close.

In the flat, cold, the damp air from outside leaking between windows mobile in their frames, through gaps in the walls and holes in the corners of the roof where birds squeeze their bodies and mice burrow. In the flat that smells of last night's meal and a slow lingering essence of something stale. Kate isn't there. She'd walked the cold, quiet Sunday streets over to her mum's house by herself. Told Matthew she wanted to go alone today. Didn't want him with her. His initial reaction was relief that he wasn't expected to go over to her mum's again. But then he'd been angry. He was the victim here. Not her. He was the one who'd been lied to and treated like a fool. And he wanted to know what was going on.

Matthew sits on the floor, one foot tucked under the opposite leg, one foot, bare, outstretched on the carpet. He sits by the open wardrobe with an open box, an old shoebox full of Kate's old junk. He'll tell himself he didn't mean to do this. It just sort of happened. He knows it's a terrible thing to do, like reading someone's diary, like seeing someone's thoughts plainly on their face and telling them so. Maybe if he'd done that with Kate though, told her he could see what she was thinking, feeling, told her he knew there was something so wrong between the two of them, maybe then he wouldn't be sitting here on the floor, while the flat was quiet, going through her little box of secrets.

Part of Matthew wants to stop right now, close the box, wrap the elastic band back around twice like she had, feel it twang and hear the noise it made as it sprang back to the stiff cardboard of the box. Part of him wants to get up off the floor and go and sit in the living room and listen as tourists walk past down in the street and cars try to shunt down the narrow road, and pretend he'd never opened the box in the first place.

Part of Matthew is a coward, and part of him wants to wring Kate's neck for doing this, to him, and to all those people at the funeral, but mostly just to him.

He found them first because they were laid on top of the other stuff when he opened the box. The box had the words *Kate's Things* written in black felt-tip on the lid, so Matthew knew it contained secrets. When he opened the box the envelopes were laid on top of a pile of other stuff. He took the first one out. It was addressed to Ms. M. Hooper. Matthew had no idea who that was, but it wasn't Kate, or anyone she knew as far as Matthew could remember. He opened the envelope and a note fell out. It fluttered to the floor beside his foot that was outstretched on the carpet. He looked at the folded piece of paper, white, and he noticed how dirty his foot looked beside it. He touched his foot first, rubbed the sole as if it was dusted with damp sand from the man-made beach further along the shore and he could work it off with his fingers. Then he moved his hand to the right and touched the note. He opened it like it might be toxic, keeping it a distance from his face. He read the words. At first he felt his eyes tense and his face tighten into an involuntary frown. This wasn't anything to do with him or Kate. *I'm sorry to tell you, but Peter died last Tuesday.* It was a letter to M. Hooper, telling her someone had died, someone who must have been close to her. *I'm sorry to tell you.* He imagined M. Hooper being upset, whoever she was. Maybe Peter was her cousin, or uncle, maybe she would cry. But then Matthew felt his face change and his stomach constrict. He tasted acid in his throat. Felt like a hurricane was coming. Peter. Kate had said, days and days ago now, Peter died. And Matthew asked *Who the hell is Peter?* And Kate never really answered. Even though they both knew very well who Peter was. Matthew suddenly experienced the sickening certainty that no one else had seen this letter. Only Kate had. She had opened it and consumed its contents. She had taken it inside of her as if it was meant for her. Who knows, maybe she had even become M. Hooper for a day or two. One thing Matthew knew for sure, Kate had gone to that funeral. She'd told him so. She dressed in black one morning and she'd told him she was going to the funeral.

She'd bought clothes and she'd gone to the funeral. As if she belonged. As if she had a right. As if she, in some way, deserved to be there. She'd actually gone to the funeral. Just the thought of that made him so angry.

*

He used to spend so many hours, thinking *what if* that now it was here it seemed so perverse. What if? He'd wound his own heart into knots thinking *what if he runs away? The dog. What if I let him off the lead one day and he goes? What will I do?* And now there was no question anymore.

Peter had begun to see the dog as the only living creature that understood. He'd begun to look upon the dog as his only true companion. The dog didn't want anything from him, only food and water. The dog didn't ask him to listen, to comply, to take charge, to sort stuff out, to cope. The dog only wanted him to be there, just like he wanted the dog to be there. It was him and the dog, and that was it. And now, now he was taking his *what if* and making himself face it. Head on.

Every morning now he took the dog outside and they stood there together, the lead hanging in Peter's grasp, the dog free. But the dog just sat there and looked up at him and waited. *What's next? What happens now?*

He looked all around him at the house and the trees and the green lawn, and the land beyond, and then he looked down at the dog.

"Go on," he said, "Go now. It's time to go now."

This was three days before he would die. The dog wouldn't go. It just stood there looking at him, its eyes dragging in its head. "Go on!" he said.

But it was no use. Susie had made the appointment at the vet's for that afternoon, but it was Peter's job to go and he couldn't face it. The dog had a tumour like a rock in its chest, and was getting slower every day with the weight of it. The vet had said there was nothing more to do now. But still Peter couldn't face it. He couldn't willingly take his dog to die at the appointed time. It wasn't natural. It would be better if he let the animal go now and he found his end out there. Unexpected. Surely that was better. But the dog wouldn't go, and Peter was just a coward.

He looked down at this loyal beast and he sighed. "OK," he said. "Have it your way." He looped the lead back around the dog's head. He took a deep breath and sighed it out. He would do it. He didn't have much choice as far as he could see.

*

Matthew hitched his body up into the van that waited at the end of the road. He slung his bag down by his feet and turned to his work-mate. "Morning," he said. The van was moving before he'd finished pulling his seat belt over his chest, the driver checking the road and turning around in the small car park by the sea. Gulls squawked in the grey air and circled tourists for any sniff of food.

"How's that girlfriend of yours?" the driver asked.

"She's OK."

The driver glanced at him to check his mood before he asked anymore. Matthew was looking at the street.

"She still off work?" the driver went on.

"Yeah, but she should be going back soon."

"What is it that's wrong with her?"

Matthew shifted in his seat. He hated having to try to explain. There were no easy phrases that covered a thing like this, no accepted answers. So he used the one that she always used. He said the things that people could nod their heads at and feel they had some understanding of.

"It's a stress thing, you know."

"Yeah. Is it work then? Loads off with that, pressure and everything at work. Loads of people having that."

"Kind of," Matthew said. He shrugged. "I don't know

though," he went on. "I mean, it is work, that is why she's stressed, but... come on, it's not like she's got a really stressful job, is it? It's not like she's under pressure."

"Yeah well, if you ask me, this whole *stress* thing is out of control. You know what people are like, they can say they're *stressed* at work and get a couple of weeks off." Matthew's work-mate turned to look at him quickly. "I'm not saying that's what Kate's doing, I didn't mean that."

"Nah, you're alright, mate," Matthew said. "To be honest I sometimes wonder if that's exactly what she's doing."

The driver dutifully nodded and directed the van towards Silver Street.

*

She knew what she was doing... didn't she? She knew exactly how he felt about her and what this would mean. But still, she went with him anyway. It was harmless. It was a bit of flirting, that was all. Everybody likes to flirt. Everybody does it. It wasn't serious. It wasn't real. Surely he knew that. He was married. Old enough to be her dad.

Peter waited for her at the end of the day. He hung around near the door and held back while she unhooked her coat in the staff room, pushed her arms in through the sleeves and said goodbye to the other women doing the same, holding up her hand in a stationary wave. She walked with Peter, out of the factory and to his car. She got in the car as if she'd done this a million times. Saw his smile as he sat down behind the steering wheel, a smile that said his luck was in, a smile that said he couldn't believe this was actually happening.

His jeep looked battered. There was mud spiked up the side of each door. The paintwork was scratched and inside receipts and empty plastic bags lay like old people on a beach, in for the day, not to be shifted. Kate must have stared at the disarray on the back seat as she climbed up and into the passenger seat of the jeep, because Peter shot a look behind him, his face rinsed by embarrassment, and he said, "Sorry, it's a bit of a mess, this old jalopy."

He patted the dashboard as he said this, and Kate could see the place in Peter's heart this vehicle occupied. Strange that, she thought, how men love engines, how they love these things that were built by other men, designed by other men, made to serve them.

"I don't usually drive this to work," he said. "But my wife has taken my other car today because hers is having its MOT…"

His wife had a car and he had another car? She thought about how much money someone would have to have to own that many cars. The thought inched its way forward in her blood. Kate and Matthew only just had enough money to cover the rent on the flat and buy food, even one car was out of the question, never mind two.

They drove to Lyme. Peter couldn't hide it. It was on his face. All over him. A creeper.

She's with me.

Peter drove the car with a slightly uneasy smile now. The next part was crucial. If he got this wrong it could all be over. He drove in towards Lyme, a bubble expanding inside him, pushing all his other feelings aside. They passed a house on the right and Kate held out her hand and pointed to it. "See that house there?" she said. "I used to think that was a real castle," she said.

Peter glanced quickly at the house. He already knew what it looked like and why she'd thought that. The house had what appeared to be a turret at one side of it, the kind of thing you might imagine a princess to be imprisoned in, a kind of tower for a beautiful damsel to let her hair down from, waiting to be rescued. Of course it was only there for appearances, but he knew what she meant. Had passed that house hundreds of times, had even thought the same thing once.

"When I was little," she went on, "I used to think that a princess lived there, and probably knights or an evil witch. Or both."

Peter smiled. It was more intimate than anything that might happen now. More personal than any of the other things she'd said to him before. Of all the things he'd taken as she spoke them and folded them deep inside himself, this one thing he would fold deeper than any of the others.

He looked at her once, twice, while he drove, his eyes flicking back to the road quickly each time. It would be OK now. That one piece of information from her childhood, that one memory, was as good as any signal.

He pulled into a quiet spot. Turned off the engine. Kate heard the fall of it in the car, a dying breath, a last sigh. She looked at Peter as he turned to her. There was no age. No difference at all. He stared into her, his eyes like natural water. As he leaned forward she realised he was actually going to kiss her, and for the first time she wondered briefly what it would be like with him, with a man of this age. Would it be different?

*

Once, when she first met Matthew, before he had the flat, when he still lived with his mum and dad, he had a car instead. He didn't own the car for long. Sold it when he moved into the flat. But for a few brief weeks he tried to impress Kate by picking her up and taking her on dates. The car was a dusty black Astra. When she slid in and sat down next to him, Matthew would put his hand on her knee firmly, his fingers stretching right around the small part of her leg just above the bone of her knee, before it became her thigh, his hand grasping. Then they would drive and go to the cinema, or just drive. The time with the car didn't last long, but she can never forget it.

They'd been to see a film and on the way back home Matthew's hand grasped her leg a little higher, pushing her dress up till her skin was visible beneath her tights. He said he knew a place, and he drove to the car park at the back of a boarded-up pub, sunken slightly in a dip. There he switched off the engine and laid back Kate's seat.

The car windows were misted over with breath and they had just opened the doors, still breathing heavy and sitting back in their own seats, when another car rounded the side of the pub and pulled up behind them.

"It's not a police car, is it?" Matt said, smiling. "Yeah, it is. Would you believe it? I'll have to go out and speak to them. But don't worry, we're not bothering anyone out here." Just as he was getting out he said, "We'll never be able to forget our first time now, will we?"

*

She looked at him again. "What are you doing?" she asked.

Peter's face gave way to a small hole in his composure. She turned her body away from him and reached for the door. Released it and slid down out of the jeep. She slammed the door shut and left him sitting there. Vibrations in the air where she had just been were all that was left. He felt the silence and emptiness and the space her body had occupied moments before. There was nothing left at all.

*

Matthew's work-mate had put the radio on loud that day. They'd had a good afternoon, a straightforward job with no complaints or last minute changes and now they were in the van, on their way home. They were both in a good mood. Rare low winter sun hit their eyes for a second as they entered Uplyme, then the clouds began to clump and it disappeared behind them. Matthew leaned forward, his seat belt straining, to tap the dashboard in front of him lightly as if it were bongos. They'd rounded the corner and Matthew's work-mate had sung along to a couple of lines blasting from the radio, when they saw her.

The jeep was a battered old thing, but it was memorable. Most people round here had brand new ones, used mainly to do the school run and nip to the shops in. Matthew could see straight away that this one was loved. Not because of the condition, it wasn't in great condition, but because it was unusual, and people who owned unusual cars tended to love them.

So why had Kate just got out of that jeep right in front of them and begun running away down the street?

"Isn't that your Kate?" Matthew's work-mate asked.

Matthew was staring at her form running down the pavement.

"Yeah."

"What's she doing up here? You want me to pull up?"

"What? No." Matthew was thinking. The music was suddenly too loud and he leaned forward and turned it down. He felt awkward. If they stopped and picked her up Matthew would have to ask her what she was doing, right in front of his work-mate. Or his work-mate would ask her, and that would be even worse.

He tried to rationalise the scene he was looking at, and his first instinct was to push it all away.

"No," he said. "She probably needs to go to the shop or something, just go on and I'll meet her back at home."

His work-mate took a sidelong glance at him, and Matthew knew in that moment he could see how skewed this was.

"OK," he answered. He turned the van down into Lyme, Kate's running form still visible along the street.

*

It was going dark when Kate walked back from her mum's house. She felt the cold winter air falling all around her and saw light from stars flick the sea down in the bay. And she thought a little time apart could perhaps be a good thing for her and Matthew. Maybe they needed to breathe for themselves like this, like she was doing now on the walk home.

She heard him move as soon as she was back inside the flat. She'd come up the stairs and unlocked the door and closed it behind her. And she heard his body slide against the wet bath sides. She locked the door and placed her keys on the kitchen table. She opened the bathroom door and stepped inside.

"Hey," she said.

He sat up. "I didn't hear you come in."

"Matt… me and you…"

He ignored her. "Who is M. Hooper?" he asked.

"What?"

"M. Hooper. The person who the invitation to the funeral was really for. Who is that?"

She knew she'd blushed. Couldn't control it. She felt around in her thoughts for how he could know about that. Maybe he'd seen it when Melanie did, but he'd never mentioned it before.

"How do you know about that?" she said.

"I found the invitation."

"Found it?"

"Yeah, when I was going through your things. You weren't invited to the funeral, but you went anyway. M. Hooper was invited."

"You went through my things?"

"I wanted to know what else you'd been hiding from me. Who is M. Hooper? And why were you so desperate to be at Peter's funeral?"

"I can't believe you would…"

But he cut her off, the same anger that pushed him too far before filling his voice. "Just answer me!"

"It's Melanie. The woman who lived here before we did. She was invited to the funeral because she… she and Anthony were together and she knew Peter."

"As well as you knew him? Just how well did you know him?"

There was a sneering in his voice that made Kate recoil. She was going to have to tell him something.

"I worked with him, you know that, and…"

"And?"

"He tried it on once."

"What do you mean? When?"

She took a deep breath, the steam from the bath filling her throat and lungs, making her feel light-headed.

"Does it matter when?"

"It matters to me!"

"He tried it on, and I knocked him back, and then he killed himself. That's it!"

Matthew leaned towards her, his whole face tensed in confusion. "What?"

"It was my fault. His death, him killing himself. It was all my fault."

Kate was sitting on the floor in the bathroom. He'd been through her things, her personal things, he'd purposefully gone looking for her guilt. Kate was struggling to square how she felt about that. It was a betrayal of her trust. She should be able to trust him. But he should also be able to trust her. And she *was* guilty, just not of what Matthew thought.

Steam from the bath filled the air. It felt hot when she breathed in and it was suffocating in the small room. Matthew just stared at her all the time she had been standing there. So she'd sat down. She looked up at him and thought his shoulders must be cold, him sitting up in the bath like that, but he was just sitting there and didn't take his eyes off her.

She waited for him to say something. Instead he ran more hot water into the bath and when he turned the tap off a whistle like a fast train came from the hot water tank in the kitchen. Kate concentrated hard on the sound and hoped it would fill the silence enough to make all this feel normal again.

Matthew stirred in the water, sending ripples all about his body. "Why didn't you tell me?" he said finally.

She shrugged. "I didn't think I should. It seemed wrong. It was nothing at first and I thought I'd just let it go, it would be better to just leave it."

He lifted his eyebrows at her.

"Well, I didn't know it would go that far, did I?" she said.

"But after," he said. "You could have told me after he'd died. Why all this secrecy, all this pretending?"

"I couldn't take it," she said. "He died. I just couldn't forget it, I couldn't let it go."

"So at least this explains what all your 'stress' has been about!" Matthew sighed. "Does anyone else know? About you I mean."

She shook her head. Held her knees closely with her arms wrapped around her legs on the floor. At least he wasn't angry now. At least she could hear compassion in his words now. He did care, she knew he did. And they'd both done things they weren't proud of.

At least she could feel the anger in his voice subsiding.

"His son, the one… Does he know?"

She shook her head more slowly this time.

"Will you tell him? Is that why…?"

She shifted uncomfortably on the floor, edging herself from side to side.

"No," she said. "I can't tell him."

"Then what have you been doing hanging around with that loser? Why? I'm trying to understand all this Kate, but really..."

"He looks just like Peter," she said. And she looked at Matthew then as if the words were alive in the air. "At first I just wanted to go to the funeral and... I don't know, you can't just crash a funeral, can you?"

"Well, you could have stood out of sight or something. If you just wanted to be at the funeral."

"I didn't just want to be at the funeral, I wanted to be in the whole thing. I wanted to... pay my respects, it sounds so corny, but I wanted to... make a kind of peace with him I suppose."

"You mean with Peter?"

"Yeah, I know it was too late, but I wanted to say sorry."

"That doesn't sound corny at all," Matthew said. "It's actually the only bit of it I can understand."

"Well, then I met Anthony and... he's so much like him, I don't know, I couldn't let go. I felt I could still make it up to Peter if I spent time with Anthony…"

She leaned forward, the meaning in what she was saying

pushing her on. "His eyes. His mannerisms. It's… weird. I had no idea all that could pass so intact from a father to their child. It's all there, bits of Peter right there as if they'd been taken from him and just put into Anthony. Do you think it's like that with everyone? Do you think our dads are that visible in all of us?"

She watched him as he listened to her, and she thought no one understood her like Matthew. She thought there was no one else she could talk to like this. Despite all the bad times lately, he was still the person she could turn to, he was still the closest person she had.

"I think you should tell him," he said. "I think you should tell Anthony about you and Peter." He could still feel the jealousy inside him. The way she tried to explain all this away didn't get rid of it. And he didn't care if nothing really happened between them, it was another man, and she'd kept it from him, because she knew how it would make him feel, because she'd felt guilty. Matthew wanted to blast the whole thing away. Get rid of it. He wanted to put it in the past and feel that he'd done something about it. Be the man. Stand up for what was his. Or at least fight back in some way.

Kate sat forward on her knees and held the side of the bath. She looked for a long time at Matthew. His eyes connected with hers. Until he said, "Someone needs to tell them what happened."

Matthew pushed his arms into his white overalls and pulled the cloth up over his back. He fastened the boiler suit down the front and took hold of his bag. Kate watched him. Saw all the colours of past jobs in lines on the cloth like the unseen marks of past loves left in someone's body. He looked at her once before turning and leaving the flat. She moved slowly over to the window and waited for him to reappear down in the street, and walk to the end of the road to wait for his lift to work. She watched his body move as he came out of the alleyway between the flats and walk out in a weave through the splutter of tourists. He'd said it wasn't finished, this business with Peter. Matthew said it wouldn't be finished until everything was straight. Kate bit the skin around her fingernails and watched him. She had no idea how this could ever be finished.

*

Monday morning. At least she didn't have to go to work too. She would take her time busying around the flat, going to the shops. Work. Just the thought filled her with dread. It wasn't just what had happened but the boring tedious nature of her mundane job filing papers and inputting invoice data.

Kate remembered staring around the dull office, feeling the drag of the working week. Strip lighting hung from the ceiling on chains. They always reminded Kate of some sort of neon swings, like she could climb up there and sit on them and dangle her feet as she swayed on them like a schoolgirl. She looked up at them sometimes, when she was avoiding looking at her work. Her work bored her to tears.

When Kate was at school she'd imagined being an air hostess or a beautician. She'd seen herself in the uniforms, a professional, glamorous, independent woman. But not many kids grow into the jobs they'd imagined at school, and once Kate had left and looked down her immediate future, she'd recognised her limitations and knew she'd never look right in those uniforms anyway.

She told herself this job was temporary. A stop-gap until she figured out what she really wanted to do with her life. She told her colleagues she had no intention of staying long, and they looked at her and smiled, placing themselves back where she now stood, saying the same words she now said. But they'd stayed. And they knew she would too.

The thought of work filled Kate with dread. But Melanie was different. She didn't feel much in the way of stress, or she dealt with it well, that's what her boss at the rope factory had said. Works well under pressure. Handles stressful situations well. And it was true. She rarely felt truly stressed.

She hadn't cared much when she left school. Just needed to get a job and didn't think too far forward. Rolled into the job carelessly and then straightened out and found ambition she'd never realised she had. She'd looked around at herself one day.

Dead end job. Nine to five. Day in day out with nothing ever happening. And she'd wondered how she could have let this happen. How did she end up here, working for the council? She realised she wanted more. More challenge, more horizons, more life. And from that day on she became the person a careers officer would actually like to have an interview with.

When Melanie was fourteen the careers officer had done the rounds at school, like they did in every other school. Each pupil waited to be called into the quiet, scary office where "the talk" would happen.

Melanie was aware of the image she projected by the way she dressed, the colour and the way she did her hair. She was aware that people saw this as some sort of defiance, but it wasn't. She had nothing to be defiant about. No axe to grind. She didn't look like this because of some need to rebel and stick it to the world, unlike Anthony, who certainly moulded himself out of anger. Melanie just felt this way. She was expressing the way she felt.

"What do you see yourself doing in five years' time?" the careers officer asked.

Really? Was that the best she could do? This woman sat next to Melanie with a file full of information and a head, surely, full of interesting possibilities, and that was the question she asked. Melanie sat back in her chair and looked at the woman. She was more nervous than Melanie. She was spooked by Melanie's hair, bleached to the colour of vanilla ice cream, and the eyeliner that Melanie had drawn on thick under her eye like an Egyptian Queen.

"I dunno," she shrugged. "Haven't really thought about it."

The careers officer didn't say much that day that was of any use to Melanie, except this one thing. "Well," she said, looking Melanie in the eyes. "Maybe it's time you did think about it."

From the window she could see the road, and beyond that she could see the bridge and the trees. There was a ditch down there that Melanie had once sat on the edge of and cried when she'd been dumped one lunch time by a short-lived boyfriend. One of the trees that overhung the ditch permanently had a length of rope tied tightly around one of its branches, dangling over the ditch like a plumb line. Younger boys used this as some sort of adventure playground. They stood on the edge of the ditch and held onto the rope, then they swung over the ditch, their young upper arms straining against the weight of their bodies, before they either made it to the other side or fell to the muddy ground beneath them. Melanie had paused her tears that day and gazed up at the way the rope had become one with the straggling branches of the trees, as if returning to nature, like everything else.

Melanie was surprised to come across the same woman at college when she was just about to take her A-levels. "You're an intelligent girl," said the careers officer, who was already placing a list of work placements on the desk in front of her. "This one here might be a good start for you."

Melanie looked down at the paper the woman had slid across the desk to her.

"Finance assistant?"

"Why not? You would learn useful skills for the future in a job like that."

"But the council?" Melanie said. "Me?" Work for the council?"

"You can do anything you want, but you have to start somewhere."

So she'd started. She'd gone for that job and she'd got it. She'd worked for the local council, something she'd thought she'd never do. She'd heard her own heeled shoes clicking on the wooden floor as she walked the corridor and she'd begun to think about what she wanted. She wanted better, and she knew what she didn't want. She didn't want to stay here in this job for ever.

After a couple of years she had gained enough experience to give her the confidence to start looking around. There wasn't an awful lot going in the town, but when the job came up for manager at the Bay Hotel she'd gone for it. Honestly, she'd never know how she'd talked her way into that one. She'd never worked in a pub, let alone a hotel, but she'd convinced them she could do it, would be brilliant at it, would be the perfect person for that job. And, she thought, let's face it, it's not like they had queues of people applying or anything.

So, she'd been lucky. Maybe. Maybe part luck, but definitely part determination. That's what had got her to where she was today. A determination to get to where she wanted to be. And Melanie wasn't going to let anyone stand in her way.

*

The white van made it up the hill. Stopped at the traffic lights at the top before turning right towards Devon. Just before the *Welcome to Devon* sign the van turned left up a secluded driveway. Matthew sat in the passenger seat and held his bag to his chest.

Matthew could feel himself tensing inside as the van cut the shape of a hood in the gravel driveway and parked up overlooking the garden. He followed on as his partner in painting and decorating, the driver, got out and stood beside the van, slamming the door and looking all around the house and garden, whistling low and shaking his head. "Would you look at this?" he said. And Matthew just nodded. "Yep," his partner went on. "Some money round here."

There was money alright, but Matthew was thinking about that woman's face, the one who lived here, when she had come round to the flat asking about Melanie, and the way that bloke, her son, Peter's son, had looked when he was slumped on the ground down in the village, not knowing what the hell was going on or why Matthew was hitting him again and again. And Peter. He couldn't help but think about Peter. Matthew felt sick. What if Anthony was here? And even if he wasn't, Susie would recognise him straight away from the flat. How could he face her?

"You alright, mate?" his partner said. Matthew forced himself to look at his partner. "Yeah fine," he said. "Come on."

Susie answered the door. She seemed to hesitate when she smiled at Matthew, as if she was searching through old memories for the one that fitted his face.

"Come in, come in," she said, and Matthew still wasn't sure if she remembered him from the flat or not. He walked slowly into the house. The discomfort worried at every inch of his body. He felt the energy drain from him as he entered and a dragging feeling of dread take its place.

She started to show them around the house, talking all the time about what she wanted doing with the place. "I want a complete overhaul. Brand new. Start again."

Matthew thought he could understand why this woman would want to do that after what had happened. He looked up as they passed through to the living room. The stairs seemed cold, so much so that Matthew found himself placing his hands at opposite elbows as if he was about to hug himself warmer again. He looked to his left and saw photos arranged on a sideboard, some in bulky ornate frames, pictures of people who were long dead, only kept alive in black and white in these images. Some colour, of people who lived in other houses now, with other families. Susie's sons, their wives and children. And Peter. Peter on a boat with Susie, on holiday, skin browned like buffed cow hide. Matthew looked back towards the kitchen and caught a stare from Susie. He held it still until embarrassment took over his body and he almost cursed himself as he looked away from her.

"Aw, damn it," his partner said. "I'm gonna have to pop back home. I forgot those new rollers that I bought for today."

Matthew nodded and his partner turned to go.

"Be as quick as I can."

*

The floor was polished until you could sense the slippery sheen just by glancing at it. Peter stood by the photocopier and glanced at the floor. He used to love Mondays. He used to love his job and never had a Sunday-night dread of the next day. When his kids were small his office on a Monday morning was a relief after a weekend of noise and stress at home. Now everything had changed, he realised. It was Monday again, but one week ago he'd offered Kate a lift home. He had a sudden feeling. One he'd never had before. A sort of a panic. He didn't fit here now, any more than he did at home. He couldn't move, couldn't risk stepping away from the safety of the photocopier. That floor had just been buffed to such an extent Peter couldn't bring himself to walk on it. He would slip. He would fall. He was sure.

The other four employees in the office were staring at their screens. Typing. Lifting a telephone. Cursing under their breaths. Peter gazed at them for a moment. They were empty spaces. They were nothing. They couldn't help him, not now. No one could help him, not even her. He'd tried to make her see, but he'd gone too far. Wrong of him to expect her to understand. Ridiculous of him to think that she would empathise with age and weariness and a need to rediscover some sort of meaning to everything. He could never have the things back that he had when he was young. No one could. What made him any different?

He honestly had no idea how he would get back to his desk now from where he was standing. This odd feeling filled him up and bled into his muscles. He couldn't move now even if he wanted to. And he didn't want to. He would break his neck on that shiny floor. He could almost feel the crack of his bones. It was crazy to try. It was suicide.

*

Susie walked slowly towards him, lightly touched one of the framed photos on the sideboard.

"I realise that redecorating might seem like a futile attempt at changing things," she said to Matthew. "But I'll give it a try. I'd rather not sell the house, so..." she shrugged, never looking up from the photo her hand rested on. "How do you know?" she asked. "About Peter...? I saw you looking at the photos and I recognise you from somewhere, but I can't…"

Matthew felt his mouth and tongue dry as he struggled to respond. How did he know about Peter? How did he *know* Peter? For a second he couldn't say anything, just stared at her, and his instincts told him to get out of there right now, just run, just leave it all and never have to face this situation. But she was looking right at him, waiting for an answer, and if he left now he'd still have to face her at some point.

"I live with Kate," he said. "Down in the village. We live in Melanie's old flat, you came round looking for Kate the other day, but she wasn't in."

Susie tilted her head back for a moment, the memory he was giving her filling up her brain. "Ah yes," she said. "Melanie's old place, of course. It would be Melanie who told you about Peter."

"No, I don't know Melanie," he said. "Kate told me."

Susie looked up at him. "What do you mean you don't know Melanie? Kate said they were close, and she lived in that flat before you. If you live with Kate you must know Melanie."

Matthew's embarrassment and unease were quickly overtaken by his temper. He could feel all his anger about this situation turn over inside him again. Sick with feeling like he'd been made a fool. Feeling like he was the only one in the dark. But he wasn't the only one. Susie didn't know the truth either. It was just as he had told Kate: *someone needs to tell them what happened.*

He looked at her now and he could see the same deep angry confusion in her skin as he had in his. For a moment he felt they had common ground.

"I've met her obviously," he said. "When I moved into the flat, but I don't *know* Melanie," Matthew paused for a second. He was still angry with Kate. He tried to persuade himself that he could let it go that easily, that he could find himself above it. But he was still angry with her. But more than that he was still angry with Peter. "And neither does Kate," he said. "She made that up. But she did know Peter. She worked with him."

Susie's face became mottled with some kind of humiliation, speckled pink and red over her neck and breastbone. "Why would she go making up a thing like that?"

"It's… complicated."

"Yes, it sounds it… but she knew Peter?"

The question rumbled about in Matthew's chest. He felt sick when he thought about it. The guy was old enough to be

Kate's dad. He was married. She was with Matthew. And yet none of that stopped him. He'd still made a play for her. Probably been after her since the minute he saw her. And she'd gone along with it. She'd carried on with this and not said a word about it to Matthew. Just like he was sure Peter hadn't said a word to Susie either. The bitterness of feeling like a fool twisted inside him.

"Yes," he said. "She knew him pretty well actually."

*

Melanie had been hearing about this girl for weeks. She wasn't actually sure which one of the office staff it was, but one of Melanie's colleagues told her something had to be done. Apparently she added five minutes onto every one of her breaks and she thought no one noticed. She hung around by the photocopier waiting for papers to slide through when she could be using her time doing something else instead. There was no need to stand there like that. No need to guard the bloody machine. There was no excuse.

This girl, Kate her name was, was taking the piss. She wasted time. She stood watching the photocopier when she could be getting on with work. She took too long getting a drink and going to the loo. And when she was back she was staring vacantly around the office. And she was distracting other members of staff. Melanie had to do something about it. She sat in her office with rotas and schedules, timelines and plans all marked out on sheets of paper. She didn't actually know who the girl was but she would move her. Maybe the work was too boring for her and the girl would respond to a new challenge. Melanie had it in her head the other people in that office were probably part of the problem and it was just like splitting apart two kids in school who talk too much. She would move her out of that office and everything would be fine; everyone could get on with their work and things would return to normal.

*

After the incident during the lift home she'd acted normal with him at work the next day, and she'd made his heart feel solid in his chest. It was odd.

A couple of other people in the office were talking about their boyfriends and one confessed to cheating.

"Yeah, but what do you define as cheating?" the other asked.

The first girl shrugged. "Cheating's cheating."

"No, it's not," the other one said. "I mean, kissing's not cheating really is it? You have to go all the way for it to be cheating. I mean, if you're out one night and you see someone else you fancy, that's nothing really, everyone does it."

Kate looked Peter right in the eyes and said, "Yeah, we all make mistakes."

He'd smiled back at her, but had no idea what to say. He wasn't sure what she meant, but one thing he was sure of, it was OK. She was making everything OK. He'd been so sure of that at the time. It didn't occur to him in that moment that what she was actually saying was, he'd made a mistake, and she wasn't going to talk to him again because of it; it was the end.

All she ever had to do was smile at him and she made all the other problems in his life, all the big stuff, shrink to the size of peach stones and lie down in his belly for a while when he was around her. She calmed him somehow. She tamed his anger and tucked it beneath his ribs so he couldn't feel it at all, just by looking at him.

But when he got back from his lunch break that day she'd been moved.

*

No matter how hard he tried for the rest of the week, he couldn't get her alone. It was almost like she was doing it on purpose, and the more he thought of that, the more he thought that was exactly what she was doing. Peter was struggling with it.

What was more, as Tuesday afternoon became Wednesday, and Wednesday became Thursday, he was getting more and more worried. He needed to find out if she'd been moved because she'd said something to someone in the company about what had happened in his jeep.

She was at the other end of the building now, where Peter wouldn't normally be "just passing". What's more she was avoiding looking at him at all. Peter tried at first to work around this problem. He tried to find excuses to go over to her desk and talk to her, but she would just glance up at him with a blank expression until he felt like the eyes of everyone in that office were stuck on him, all waiting, all watching, and Kate's were the most accusing of all. She'd raise her eyebrows as if to ask, what do you want? And he'd feel himself crumble. She wanted to avoid him. It didn't take a genius to work that out.

He spent the whole week trying to leave messages for her, asking other members of staff to pass them on. Emailing her. But she never answered. Peter was left with the agonising pastime of replaying in his head every moment he had spent with her. The way her blonde hair fell like ripples on water around her face. Her eyes, slightly upturned at the corners. Her mouth. The shape of her shoulders and the shade of her skin. Every look. Every smile. Until he felt like his whole body was so used and drained by these repetitions he just didn't have the energy to keep on doing it anymore. She was just an excuse, he knew that. That girl, Kate, she was just a girl. He knew it wasn't love. Love didn't kill a person. Love doesn't bring a person's life right down to nothing. He didn't even know what love was anymore, wasn't even sure if it existed at all. But she was a cure. He had nowhere else to turn. Nothing else he could do. He looked all around himself, but couldn't see a route he could take to get him out.

It was a strange kind of sickness. An invisible emotional sickness. If he'd felt there was something physically wrong with him he would have known what to do. He would have dealt with it. Like he had done with the dog a few years ago when it had started being sick in the night. Peter had wasted no time in getting an appointment for the dog. The vet had looked the animal over and made him better. Treated it. Put things right. That was what he himself needed.

Unfortunately Peter had another appointment with the vet this weekend, and there was nothing that could be done this time except put the dog out of its misery. But at least it was something. It was better than nothing. At least there was a person there who knew exactly what to do.

Peter wished there was someone he could turn to like that. He wished there was somewhere he could go, someone he could see to get himself sorted out or find out if his condition was terminal. But he couldn't. He couldn't go to a doctor. There was nothing *actually* wrong with him. It was all just in his head, in his heart, it was inside himself. Peter felt there was only one person who could help him.

Kate. Herself.

But it was already the end of the week and he still hadn't managed to get her alone.

*

Susie had been watching her husband's face for the confusion that overtook it now and then. She had caught glances of pain bleeding through his skin and struggling in his eyes. And she had felt something, just felt something that was very wrong, something coming, unstoppable, something that was growing inside Peter. Something she could do nothing about. She had tried to talk to him, but Peter had answered with a smile. So she kept watching him. She saw him sigh and a deep tussle with a thought appear on his face for a moment. It scared her. It actually scared her. And she feels so stupid for that now. Such an idiot for letting a simple fear get in the way. She'd pushed hard to get rid of it. Was it her fault? Had she done something wrong? Was there someone else? Again? She almost moaned out loud when she allowed herself to think that. Not again.

*

Susie had been touching the photo frame and looking down on it as Matthew spoke. She couldn't look him in the eye. He spoke about Kate and how she had worked with Peter and how he'd become *interested* in her. He said it in such a way as to make it sound almost routine. Innocent. Like a person might be interested in a never before seen picture, or a new car, or a house. He saw the blood rise in her face and her jaw clench.

"Of course I knew there was something..."

He had realised that it would be humiliating for her. But she needed to know.

Then she breathed in deeply and held her body straighter and her head higher. "But men of Peter's age often go through these *phases*," she went on. "I could tell something was going on, you know what it's like, I ignored it. Told myself I was imagining it. Being stupid. I mean, at his age! But I knew really. Can't say I'm that surprised to find out it was her. She's young, blonde, pretty..."

"But nothing..."

"Why wouldn't he?"

"They didn't actually..."

"Well, that's not necessarily the important bit, is it?"

"No," he answered. "You're right, it isn't."

For a moment Matthew had no idea what else to say. He'd gone and done it. Had been sure it was the right thing to do. They deserved to know. At least *she* deserved to know. This woman, Peter's wife, had a right to know. Had to have some sort of rights to this information... didn't she?

He felt uncomfortable now. Stupid for thinking it was his place to tell about these intimate details that had nothing to do with him anyway.

"I just thought you'd want to know," he said. "I just thought you should know."

He could see her bent head. The redness in her skin had crept up her cheeks to cover her and had turned the colour of a new bruise. Her head flashed upwards and she caught him with one angry look.

"Did you?" she said. "On top of everything else, you thought I should know this? He was under too much pressure at work, couldn't handle being overtaken by Anthony's girlfriend when it came to promotion, beaten to it by a woman half his age, couldn't live with the fact that his youngest son had lost his job and his licence and everything through drink-driving… not to mention the money, the debt we were in that I only found out about after he'd died, and *you* thought it would be better for me to know this. You thought I would want to know *this!*"

Matthew hesitated. He thought he would probably never speak to this woman again. He thought she would blank him if she saw him in the street, which in such a small place was highly likely. He wondered if they'd passed each other before, if they had waited in the same queue in the supermarket or stood by the bar at the same time in the Pilot Boat Inn. They would never have known they were connected in this way, through these people, and now, if he saw her again, if they glanced up at each other while buying a newspaper in the sweet shop on the corner by the sea, or if they each saw the other walking the narrow streets near the Cobb, she would either turn away and deny she knew him at all, or she would stare into his face and dare him to acknowledge her. He'd brought something into her life, into her head, that she would rather not have known. He'd changed her life for ever.

"I'm sorry," he said. "I just thought… you seemed so *together.* You I mean, just you, you seemed to have everything under control and it felt wrong that you didn't know."

"What are you talking about? You thought I shouldn't be *allowed* to have things under control? But how do you know if I had everything under control or not? You don't even know me."

"No, no, I don't, I'm sorry, you're right... I just..." He paused, looking at her. "I can see that this is a shock."

Susie shook her head and turned sideways, still looking back at him. "Oh, it's not a shock," she said. "It's not a shock at all. But I bet it was a shock for you."

He peered at her, the creeping thought that maybe she knew more about him than he'd realised, that maybe she could see right through him. "Yes," he said. "It was actually. I mean I knew about Peter, and that he had… died, Kate showed me the letter, but..."

Susie frowned. "What letter?"

"The one in the Christmas card. The one you sent to the flat. The one addressed to Melanie."

He could see the memory of the note in the Christmas

card fall into place in Susie's brain. She almost laughed. "So she opens other people's mail as well, does she?"

Matthew felt a sudden rush of protectiveness. He couldn't have anyone else talking about Kate like that. She was his. She was still his.

"She's been under a lot of pressure," he said. "Stressed."

"She's been stressed?" Susie answered. Her voice was rising again, her face itching with another blush. "She has no idea what stress is. No idea what it's like. I had to deal with him, dying, the way he did it, then finding out about the money."

"Money?"

It had slipped out again. She was so angry, so bloody angry with Peter for doing this. Even now he was dead he was still causing her trouble and anxiety and worry. She'd said it before she'd realised, before she had a chance to stop herself. And now this boy was standing there looking at her for an explanation. She sighed. What did it matter anyway? What did it matter if everyone knew? It didn't even matter anymore. The whole village would probably know about it soon enough anyway.

"We were in debt up to here." She held her hand up to her neck and jutted it into the air. "Only I didn't know. He never told me. So don't tell me *she* was under pressure. She thinks she's stressed? She doesn't know anything."

*

His car was shining in the sun in the car park. Peter had always bought new cars, had always felt the pride of driving them home and seeing them glisten where people could admire them – in the factory car park, outside his house. They spoke of his achievements. But now, after Anthony had written his last one off, and with money a problem that he'd never known before, for the first time ever he'd had to buy a second-hand car. It said everything, he thought. He worried every morning that it wouldn't start. He worried about things going wrong and how he would pay for them. Just more things to add to the list of things he thought too much about. Money. His family. His age. Time. How big, and yet how small, the world was. The field beyond the back garden. The sea down the hill, opening up and going on and on. Peter could imagine how unending that must have seemed to his ancestors, when they knew no better, when they believed their own piece of land was all there was and the sea went on for ever, to the end of everything. His mind was wandering again. He couldn't concentrate on anything anymore. Didn't see the point in trying. And there was nothing in life he looked forward to anymore. It was Friday, but weekends had nothing to offer him anyway, and this weekend all he had planned was mourning both before and after his visit to the vet.

He was relieved to be getting away from Melanie and Bridport, towards Lyme. He tried to focus on his driving.

But there was one thing he couldn't get out of his mind. The expression on Kate's face. He had tried one last time to get her alone, invited her to come to the conference room to discuss something he had waffled about sales data analysis, the best idea he could come up with. Been stared down in front of everyone. Humiliated by one of the most junior employees in the company.

Then he drove past the house on the bend in the road that Kate had said reminded her of a fairy tale castle. He glanced at the house as he passed, the tower-like structure on one end of the house embedded in Kate's mind as the prison for a princess.

Kate, the way she'd talked in the car that day, the look on her face then, the one that he would have wanted to remember for ever: the reason he'd stopped, every corner of him wanting her, turned his body towards her. And she had looked at him like he was mad. Must be crazy. To think she would want him. A face that would haunt him for ever. And today it was almost the same expression when he'd said what he said to her.

That was that face that he couldn't get out of his mind. A face that told him there was no cure.

*

Susie had walked quickly from the front door. Five minutes ago Peter had come home from work, said, *I didn't get it,* and walked straight back out. She'd stood there in the house, looking down on the framed photos in the hall by the bottom of the stairs. A marriage captured and held down beneath glass. A shared life potted and made neat, all the stray, awkward parts ignored and swept away.

Men were so hard to understand sometimes. He didn't want to talk about it, but what was she supposed to do?

She waited those few minutes and then she followed him out of the door. She found him round the back of the house, standing at the head of the lawn just staring down the garden, hands in his trouser pockets, rocking slightly on his heels, only moving to throw a ball down the garden for the dog, then bending to ruffle its ears when it brought the toy back.

"Never mind," she said. "It doesn't matter." And she knew instantly that it was the wrong thing to say. Peter gave a desperate short laugh, wrapped inside his smile, and he looked up at the sky.

Of course it mattered. She had no idea, didn't understand anything. She'd never had to deal with the big stuff. Money. The house. He dealt with that. Men were supposed to deal with that. Men were supposed to make it all work, keep it all ticking along. Have it covered.

Peter continued looking up at the clouds moving slow over the sky like river water. He'd done all he could, but it wasn't enough. He'd done his best to make a start at digging him and Susie out of the financial mess they were in after all the repairs they'd had to do to the roof of the house. It would still have been hard, it would still have been a struggle to pay everything off, but it would have been a step in the right direction. And he couldn't even get that right. He couldn't cover it. Melanie had it. Not only did Peter's last chance to save all this miss by a mile, but Melanie had it, his son's girlfriend. It couldn't get much more humiliating than that.

He saw a plane shoot high over his head and disappear behind the wispy summer clouds, soundless from down here, graceful. Then he turned and looked at the house and the cars and the ground beneath his feet. None of this belonged to him now. It never really did. Nothing ever really belongs to anyone, not really, but at least he'd been able to say it did. He'd worked for it. He'd provided. He done what a man should do, even though he'd known for years there was no way he could keep up with it on what he earned at the rope factory. Now it was too late. This had been his only chance.

The latest letter from the bank was staring at him. For the last few months, ever since Melanie had got the job and Peter had let the mortgage payments slip, he'd been getting letters just like this one. He held the envelope in his hand, wondering whether he should just destroy it. Maybe he should ask Susie to open it. But he knew he couldn't do that, couldn't face the look she'd give him and the things she'd say if she found out how much trouble they were really in. She loved this house. It would kill her to have to sell it. He looked back down to the ground and felt his loneliness pool. Before, he at least had the dog with him, waiting for his movements, sitting obediently by his side or walking with him. Always there. Now he didn't even have that. Now, without the dog, he was completely alone.

When he woke up on the Tuesday, Susie curled away from him beside him in the bed like a sea-smoothed shell. He glanced over at the bedside clock. The alarm would go off in ten minutes, telling him he had to get up, get dressed, go to work. He closed his eyes and thought, what's the point in getting up? He almost laughed, it was such a cliché, but, really, what was the point?

*

"Where the hell has Peter gone?"

Melanie had seen his car in the car park that morning so she knew he was at work today but now she was at his desk and he'd gone off somewhere. Melanie had the notion she had to be tougher on him than anyone else. She understood that this was awkward for him, but he had to accept it.

The remaining staff in the office glanced round at her and shrugged. She sighed. This place was getting so tiresome. Peter had disappeared. He couldn't just disappear like that. It was only 11 o'clock. If he needed to go somewhere he had to check it out with Melanie first, he knew that. She walked over to the window and looked out at the car park. What on earth was he playing at? There he was now standing by his car. She sighed again. This was probably him trying to get one over on her, trying to show her he didn't need to ask permission from her for anything, trying to prove he was the big man. Well, she thought, we'll see about that.

*

Matthew walked out of the house and saw the van coming up the drive, his work-mate driving carefully on the gravel-covered ground. He tightened his mouth and held his hand up to his work-mate to signal for him to stop. Then he walked to the van, opened the door and got in.

"What are you doing?"

"We're off the job, mate."

"What? What are you talking about? Why?"

He looked uneasily towards the house and saw Susie peering out of the window at them.

"Just drive, alright?"

His work-mate turned the van around, the tyres crunching tiny stones, a look of bewilderment on his face.

"What happened?"

They were heading back down towards the road now, the house disappearing behind them.

"We had a... disagreement."

"A disagreement? About what?"

"She didn't like my... attitude."

"What are you talking about? What did you say? Bloody hell, Matt, how did you manage to get us kicked off the job before we've even started?"

"It was his house! Alright?" Matthew was raising his voice now. His work-mate looked to him then back to the road in front of them quickly. "Whose house?"

"That bloke. Remember? That bloke we saw Kate with

that time, in that layby. The one with the jeep."

He could see his work-mate frowning, his mind trying to make sense of what Matthew was saying.

"So... what? You jump to conclusions or something? God, Matt, you didn't go and tell her about that, did you? Tell me you didn't say that to the woman."

Matthew looked away, out of his side window, his face burning with anger and embarrassment. "It doesn't matter what I said, or what..." he said. "We're off the job and that's it."

Matthew had pulled his overalls down over his body as he walked through the flat, stepped out of them in the kitchen doorway and scooped them from the floor, bundling them in his arms and walking through to the bedroom. He pushed them half-heartedly into the wash basket and turned around in the room. The bed was neatly made, cream-coloured sheets pulled up to the neck of the pillows. He looked over the bed and then down to the floor. The rope was just visible, poking a loop of its body out from beneath the bed like the nudging, teasing edge of a lie. He bent down, one leg held straight out behind him like a dancer, and he pulled the rope from its hiding place. He passed its rough, taut body through his hands, sturdy where it was still knotted. He watched how it moved, the curve of it sliding as if it was made of bone and muscle. Then he dropped it onto the bed, just a faint flicking thought for later, and he went back into the kitchen.

Kate was setting the table. She leant over as she placed knives and forks at either side and Matthew could see how her body stretched beneath her clothes. He sat down and watched while she turned to the worktops, then bent to pull pizza from the oven, her buttocks pushing out beneath the fabric of her jeans. She turned around again, didn't look at him, but brought the pizza to the table and sat down.

They were quiet for a moment, both eating and looking at each other in short, stunted glances.

"You wouldn't believe where I've been working today."

Her face became an open question and she said, "Where?"

He hesitated, then picked the pizza up in his fingers, waited like that with it held in the air and said, "That house, where Peter lived, you know, where that bloke lives you… But it wasn't him, it was his mum, Susie. I spoke to her and…" he moved the pizza a little closer to his mouth and let the words go just before he bit into it, saving him from having to say anymore, "I told her," he said.

Kate looked up at him quickly. "You told her? About me and…?"

He swallowed hard and let his hand fall on to the table beside the plate. "It wasn't your fault, Kate."

He could see a fire somewhere in her face, under her skin, starting fast.

"I can't believe you told her!" she said. "How could you?" Her face was pinched now, her brow tight. She shook her head a little and he could see her breathing deepen.

Matthew tried to calm her. He reached out his hand to touch her arm, but she pulled away.

"How could you do that? Now, she'll think..."

"It wasn't your fault," he insisted.

"You don't know that." She emphasised each word, as if he knew nothing.

"Yes, I do," he answered. They stared at each other. He had the upper hand in that one moment. He'd spoken to the woman. He knew the things she'd said, as well as the things Kate had told him. He felt he had control. "She told me," he went on. "He was relying on that promotion at work so he could pay his debts. They were going to lose the house, and it's a big house." He shrugged.

A silence stood in the air between them for a tugged moment. He watched her as her anger dealt with the things he was saying, about Susie, about Peter.

"I'm telling you. Whatever you might think, it wasn't your fault."

She took a breath. Still didn't look up. "So... he was in debt?" she said. "And she says that's why..."

Matthew nodded. "That's what she said, yes."

He could almost see the relief running through her, slowly. It was having a calming influence on the fire that had started raging behind her eyes earlier. It was what she needed to hear. That Matthew knew for sure that it wasn't her fault.

*

Matthew could feel Kate's anger still present all evening. He'd lived with her long enough to know when to back off. Women were like that. You had to leave them be sometimes. You had to let things settle. You had to know when to pick your moment and how to approach it. Even then, it was unfathomable.

They slept that night with a crackle of tension between them. Matthew left it alone. When Kate fell asleep first he felt relief at letting it go for a while.

The next morning she spoke when she had to and he could feel the problem fraying in every move she made. But it was easing. And Matthew had all the time in the world. He wasn't going anywhere.

She'd argued with Matthew last night. Well, not an argument, but she'd been angry and it was all because of Peter and his family. All because of what happened. She could see now how she'd let it have such a negative effect on her. She could see how she'd allowed that to happen. And Matthew was right, it wasn't her fault. Maybe she'd had no part in what Peter did at all. He'd had money worries, debt, and Matthew was right, that was enough to push a man like Peter over the edge. She wanted to let it go and move on. More than anything she wanted to leave the whole thing behind. As long as it was her and Matthew together she could. They could.

When he came home from work that evening she could feel the tension left over from the night before, and she felt tired of it. It would be so much simpler if they could just go back to how things were before.

She went into the kitchen to make him a cup of tea. He followed her in and she looked at him; the way his T-shirt rounded his shoulders, his brown hair always messy, his feet in old blue socks, one toe poking through a hole in the end.

He took out a pan and dropped pasta into it, without a word. She just watched him, the way he stood, angled forward slightly watching the pans, his eyelashes just visible in the turn of his head. He was everything she wanted, and she needed to put everything else aside now.

She stood next to him, leaning against the sink.

"So, when you spoke to Susie yesterday, what else did she say?" she asked after a while.

Matthew thought through the things Susie had said, put some aside, chose which he should and shouldn't tell Kate. Thought about how she'd feel, what she'd look like, what she'd say. He began serving the pasta onto plates and carried it to the table. They sat down together.

"She just said about the debts and about how stressed he was by some things to do with his work. She said it had all got too much for him."

It brought a rumble of emotion. Poor Peter. For the first time Kate thought of him with pity.

"I can't imagine how he must have felt," she said. "To think you have no... other option, but..."

"People say it's selfish," Matthew said. "Suicide. But I suppose he thought he was doing everyone a favour."

"Suppose he did."

"At least you know it wasn't anything to do with you now." Matthew said.

"Yes," she said. "I do. I do feel better about it now."

They finished eating and moved over to the sink together, where they washed and put away the dishes. Then they turned to face each other. He put his arms around her and pulled her small body towards his. She reached her arms around his neck and shoulders, looking into his eyes. He leaned forward and kissed her. Then he stood up straight, feeling relief, and something drift from him.

"Are we OK?" he asked.

She saw his head tilt back slightly as if bracing himself

against the answer.

"We're OK," she said.

It was strange. They'd been together ages now, but that moment before he had kissed her just now had felt like it could break. Like it was the first time he'd ever tried it and he didn't know what it would be like or if she'd respond or slap him. But she'd kissed him back, her tongue finding his easily, and now he felt his body relax. It was OK. It would be OK.

He took her hand from her side and moved away slightly. "Come on," he said. He led her to the bedroom and they stood for a moment, then Matthew leaned to one side and picked up one of the pieces of rope, hardly having to look at it, stretching out his hand and feeling it solid in his palm.

Matthew touched Kate's thick hair, lifted away from her head in clumps by its weight. He held the rope down by his side with his other hand. He looked into her eyes. Brown like the woods. Like living things in earth. He stroked her hair down to her shoulder then he brought the rope up and, with both hands now, laid it around her shoulders. He took one of her hands and brought it up to touch the edge of the rope, and he took her other hand in his and placed it on the zip of his old green combat trousers. Then he unfastened her jeans, and slipped his hand inside, reaching down under her. He kept his contact with her eyes all the time and he watched for any wavering of the uncertainty in her face.

He trailed the rope from around her shoulders, let it slither like a slow word, let it fall from her shoulder like a heavy sigh to the floor. He trailed his free hand over her face and smoothed her hair down tightly on her head. Then he took her hair behind her head in his hand and held it.

He loosened his grip and glanced to the floor where the rope lay curled around itself on the bare floorboards. Unsure if he should pick it up again.

Kate put her arms around his neck, her face close to his. "We don't need…" she said. "Anything else."

He waited for the pause to stretch. "We don't need it, do we?" he said.

*

Anthony had got up that morning, that last morning of Peter's life, and he'd been in a bad mood.

It's no excuse. He knows that, but still, he'd never imagined that his words would have such an effect.

Peter was standing in the kitchen when Anthony went downstairs. He was staring into the sink as water from washing dishes swirled around and down the plughole.

He turned his body halfway around as Anthony slumped into a chair at the kitchen table.

"You were late in last night," Peter said.

Anthony sighed. Not again. He was on his case again. Why couldn't he just give it a rest? "And?" he said.

Peter shrugged. "Nothing," he said. "Just commenting. Suppose you were out with Melanie."

"What of it?"

Anthony could see Peter's face in his half turn, the way the edges of his mouth turned down before he spoke, the tension in his shoulders, in his whole body. He could almost see the irritation his presence was causing Peter.

"Surprised you two are still seeing each other, that's all, after everything that's gone on."

"Well we're not. Anyway what do you mean, everything that's gone on? You mean because she got promoted and you didn't? You think I'd finish with her over that?"

Peter turned fully around now and leaned back against the sink. "Actually no, I didn't mean that, though now you mention it, the business with that job is an indicator of how heartless she can be."

"Heartless? I'm not sitting here and listening to you call Melanie heartless. You don't know her!"

"Of course I bloody know her! And I know you. Look at all the trouble, smashing up my car for a start, while bloody drunk. Bloody drunk driving. Why didn't she stop you? She could have told you to not drink, or at least to not drive."

"Is that all you care about? Your stupid car?"

"You could have been killed!"

Anthony got up from the chair and began to walk out of the room. "Don't pretend you care about that!" he said. "You wouldn't care if I was dead!" He strode into the living room, towards the front door, and he called back just before he left the house altogether. "And I wouldn't care if you were dead either!"

*

He drove to work that day with the feeling in every corner and space of his body. He himself wouldn't care. Anthony wouldn't care. Susie wouldn't. They'd be relieved. They'd be glad he was gone. Peter stumbled through the people in his life, rolling over each one in his mind, and he couldn't think of a single person who would be sorry if he was dead. The only living creature who would have missed him was his dog. And the dog was already gone.

He tensed his hands on the steering wheel. He could see the rope factory up ahead, the place he would turn his car and park, like he did every day. No one here would miss him. He was a joke here these days. A loser. There was only one person here who'd showed him the slightest hint of treating him like a real human being and even she had been ignoring him... but still, maybe *she* would care. The thought brought a small lift in his body. Only something small. Probably nothing. But she was the only person. She'd talked to him and smiled and she'd acted like he wasn't such a waste of space after all. Kate. Maybe Kate would care.

*

She'd thought about telling Matthew, but Kate had decided to keep this one to herself. The last mis-shaped piece of the puzzle she and Peter were a part of. She'd been holding it behind her back for weeks now, watching it from the corner of her eye as it lay motionless just to one side. She might have told Matthew what she'd done – or rather, what she hadn't done – especially when he'd looked at her with such confusion over her doctor's visits and the time off work. She'd stared into his eyes sometimes and she'd felt the guilt of keeping this secret from him, piled on top of the guilt she already felt over Peter. Just living with Matthew, day in day out, she could barely stop herself from letting the truth leak out from her body. She could feel it pull at her insides again and again.

She'd even been ready to tell Anthony, but he hadn't asked her *how* she could have stopped him and really, what was the point now? Some things are better this way. Sometimes it's better to keep things between two people, and not let them out.

The more she thought about it, the more relieved she was: she was so glad she hadn't told anyone. Trust is like fog, or clear air, you can't hold it in place.

So she still hadn't told anyone, and she never would.

*

Peter had turned up at work that last day, but he'd not stayed long. He clocked in and went to his desk. Turned on his computer and looked just like he did any other day. Then he'd put his head in his hands and he'd sunk down on the desk. No one seemed to pay him any attention and when he looked up and saw the other people in the office staring at their screens and not even seeing him, something had clicked into place inside him. He'd gone to Kate's desk to find her, but she wasn't there. He'd felt a panic clench his insides. If she wasn't there... Peter didn't think there was anyone else he could say this to. He didn't know what he'd do if he couldn't try to tell her. He moved slowly back to his own desk. No one seemed to have noticed. Then in the grip of more urgent panic he went back to where Kate should be. She wasn't there, but this time he noticed her shoulder bag sitting limp on the floor by her chair. She was there in the building somewhere.

He went and sat down again at his own desk for a minute. At first the thought of her being there in the building somewhere comforted him. Then he looked at the people around him again. Nobody cared. Why did he think she would? No one would even notice. He'd stood up. Stayed like that for just a second. Then he'd turned and walked out. He walked down the stairs and out of the building. He'd walked to his car. He even opened the car door and sat inside. He was sure he was going to leave right then and do it. He was going to do it. But something was unfinished. Something brought the slightest edge of doubt. He sat with his arms outstretched, hands on the steering wheel, his whole body tensed. Then he got out of the car and went back into the factory. He couldn't do it without trying one last time to find his only cure. Kate.

He'd walked into reception and he'd put his hands on the desk, and he'd looked straight at the woman sitting on the other side and he'd said, "I need to know where Kate White is."

The woman had looked at him for a moment, her mouth stuttering with what she should say, what she should do. But Peter didn't care anymore.

"I just need to know where she is," he said. "She's not at her desk, and there's just something I need her for right now." He leant back away from the desk and stood up straight. He'd spooked the woman, he could see that, but he was sick of playing around.

"Can't you just put a call out for her?" he demanded.

She picked up the phone and held it in the air, looking at him as if she was looking at a ghost.

There seemed to be a moment then, before she slowly pressed a button on the phone, that felt as if it might never end. He waited and he tried to not think of anything else. Then he heard her speaking Kate's name into the handset. Her words travelled out into the factory, spreading like disease through the air.

She put the phone back down. "If you'd like to wait..."

But he turned and left the office without another word.

He walked straight out and stood by the doors. He saw her through the window, coming down the staircase and into reception, her blonde hair tucked behind one ear, her eyes aimed lazily at the woman behind the desk. The woman spoke something and motioned to Peter standing outside. She looked up and Peter saw her hair, her eyes, her mouth, her small body, all exactly as they'd always been, but for some reason none of it registered in the way it used to. He saw a small curl of alarm enter her face, and then she walked over and pushed the door open. "I need to speak to you for a minute," he said. She didn't question this at all. Just stared up at him.

"What's up?" she asked.

She was so small next to him. So doll-like, it empowered him somehow. "Come with me for a minute and I'll tell you," he said.

Kate glanced behind her at the office. "But..."

"It'll be fine," he said. "It's just for a minute."

They walked to the car park together and it struck Peter that this was probably the closest they'd ever been. Forget that time in the car. Forget all the other times when he'd stood by her desk, and the night in the pub when he'd touched her fingers for the first time. This, right now, was the only moment they'd shared anything real.

They stood by his car in the car park. She looked up at him, waiting to find out what all this was about.

Peter was nervous now, the energy of his emotions and his words running around under his skin.

"I'm going to kill myself," he said.

He'd expected shock, worry, maybe even some desperation and guilt, but instead she instantly pinched her face in annoyance. "What? What are you talking about?"

He could see that she didn't believe him, that she was angry he'd brought this to her and thrown it at her.

"I've thought about how to do it and I'm going to. It's over."

"Don't be ridiculous," she said. But she wasn't compassionate. She wasn't going to try and talk him out of it. She hated him now. "That's ridiculous. Why would you say that?"

"I'm just telling you."

"Why? Why would you tell me a thing like that?"

"Because you're the only person I can tell."

He saw then, after his words were out, just how things really were. She was the only person he could tell, but the thought that the two of them were in any way that connected was absurd to her.

She looked up at him, this small, naïve girl, just before she walked away and back into the building, and she said, "Don't be so selfish Peter."

And he stood there by his car, thinking, that's the first time she'd ever said his name.

She sat in the office with a pen between her fingers, knocking it repeatedly against the desk. Her eyes roamed the computer screen in front of her. She could see the figures, the sparse words, the lines made on the screen and the cursor flashing, but none of it was going in.

Did he mean it?

Did he?

Could he really mean to do it?

She shook her head as the questions crowded in. He didn't mean it. He was just trying to get a reaction from her. Emotional blackmail. A guilt trip. Whatever. He had this idea that they were closer than they actually were. Had a connection or something. He wasn't really going to do it.

Was he?

She sat there for another ten, maybe fifteen minutes, knocking the pen on the desk, shoving her hair behind her ears, staring pointlessly at the screen, putting her hands to her head and rubbing her own temples. And then she couldn't stand it anymore. What if he did? What if he really meant it and he had every intention of going through with it? What if she was the only person who knew? The only person who could stop him?

*

He watched Kate walking purposefully back into the building, then he got in the car. That was it. What was the point in staying there? What was the point in working anymore? There was nothing left to work for in his life. She was right. He'd been selfish. Why would anyone care about him now? He could live for years yet, he knew, but why bother? He would only die in the end anyway. There was no purpose to his life, he realised and it sank deep inside him somewhere. It settled. There was no point.

*

Now he was feeding a variety of different ropes through his hands. He had felt all strengths, all thicknesses, had seen all colours, pass through his fingers. He knew about rope. Had worked with it, directly and indirectly for more than thirty years now. He knew rope. Knew what it could do. Knew its capabilities and how it held up in different situations. Knew it was reliable for whatever purpose you chose for it. For instance, Peter knew that harsh manila rope was used for ship rigging and construction, while soft, almost luxurious wool was used for church bell ropes. He knew how and why climbing rope stretches when it is weighed down by a person's body. He knew the type of rope fishermen used. He knew and understood their knots. Could identify any rope, he boasted, just by looking at it.

So he knew which one to choose.

*

She got to her feet suddenly and stared around the office. The other two people in there, one man and one woman, had their faces directed at their screens and didn't seem to notice her standing up. She thought they probably presumed she needed the loo or was getting a drink. Suddenly what they thought, or what anyone else thought, didn't matter. He could be dead already.

The door closed slowly behind her as she rushed out of the office. Downstairs she found the same woman sitting at reception as before. She glanced at the woman briefly as she realised she had no idea what to do next. She ran outside and to the car park and stood there stupidly looking at where his car had been half an hour ago. It wasn't there now. He'd gone. Of course he'd gone.

Kate could feel the cold winter air stinging her skin. She stood in the space where his car had been only half an hour ago. Put her hands to her head and her fingers to her scalp through her hair. It felt like the world was moving. Like she could actually feel it. It felt she was the only thing standing still and everything else was moving.

Running back to reception she felt the panic begin to suffocate her. The air seemed colder as it rushed by her ears. She reached the door and pushed hard. Then she was at the desk again, the woman looking at her in an alarmed way.

"Peter!" she said. "The man who was here before, who you called me down for. I need to know where he lives."

The woman just looked at her.

"You don't understand! I need to know, it's an emergency."

The woman was staring at her now as if she was mad. "I can't."

"Please! Give me his address!"

"No," the woman said. "*You* don't understand. I don't have the personal details of staff members. You have to ask up at Human Resources for that."

Kate could feel the panic in her own face, making her flesh feel slack and her mouth tremble.

"But I doubt they'd give it to you," the woman was saying. "They can't just go giving out addresses like that."

*

Melanie had leant her head against the window. She could see Peter down there in the middle of the car park. What was he standing there for? Just staring vacantly at the main entrance. She left the window and ran down the stairs. Passed the woman sitting at reception who looked up sharply as Melanie came through the door. Ignored her. Went straight out into the cold mid-morning air and saw him climbing into his car. He hadn't noticed her and she knocked on his window. She frowned at him as he wound the window down.

"What are you doing?" she asked.

Peter looked at her blankly. Like he wasn't there. Like he'd been diluted.

"Where are you going?" she went on. "It's not even lunch time."

He put his hands on the wheel now, straightened out his arms, rigid, and bent his head into the space between his inner elbows. Melanie was watching him, frustration stacking up inside her. He had no respect for her at all. Didn't want to recognise that she was now in a senior position. Couldn't bring himself to do it. But Melanie couldn't let him off. How would that look to everyone else who worked there?

She stared into the car and saw a box on the passenger seat. She could see rope like a sway of silent snakes curled in the box.

"What are you doing with that?" she asked. "Peter for God's sake, will you just answer me?"

He looked up. Sighed. "What?" he said.

"Did you take that rope?" she asked. "What are you doing with it? You can't just take stuff off the premises like that, it's stealing."

He gave a pathetic laugh.

"You think it's funny?" Melanie was getting angry now. Her frustration with this man was reaching deeper into her and she could feel a kind of rage turning over in her middle.

He turned to face her and just looked at her. It made her boil. "You need to get back inside," she said. "Right now, and get back to work."

He was calm when he spoke, and it only made Melanie more angry. "Nah," he said. "I'm not doing that."

"You're not doing that?" she screamed. "Then what the fuck are you doing? You swan out of here with a box of stock just like that. What the fuck are you doing? Do us all a favour Peter and go and take that rope and fucking hang yourself."

*

She ran up the stairs and into the corridor. She'd only been to Human Resources a couple of times, but she knew where the office was, and she ran straight to it now. She could feel the well-kept carpet slightly spongy under her feet as she ran down the corridor, the walls at either side of her feeling too close.

She reached the room and burst straight in, not waiting to knock or be allowed entrance. Inside the room a thin woman with lank hair looked up suddenly as Kate ran in. Kate lunged forward and put her hands on the desk, out of breath and desperate.

"I need to know where Peter lives," she said.

The woman just looked at her, shocked by the intrusion and trying to work out what was going on.

"Peter," Kate said again. "He's in his fifties, been here years, you must know."

The woman nodded. "Yes, I know who Peter is, but I'm afraid I can't give you his address."

Kate felt impatience rush inside her middle. "You have to!" she shouted. The woman's face jolted and Kate tried to control herself. "I'm sorry, but you have to do something. He's... ill. He's ill. He's gone home, but there's no one with him. Someone has to get there, to his house!"

The woman looked slightly afraid. She nodded. "Yes, alright," she said. "We'll have a contact on file. I'll have a look."

*

Peter touched the turquoise nylon rope. It was bundled like a bale of hay and tied with string. He unwrapped a length of the rope and ran it through his hands as if he was about to cast it out and lasso someone, something. He looked ahead at where the rope would go if he did that. There was just an empty space. Beyond that a man worked a forklift like it was an extension of his limbs, part of him. Peter envied that man for a moment. He seemed to be at one with his task. Knew what he was doing. Didn't feel an ache in the pit of his stomach at the thought of having to do it.

Peter watched as the forklift moved, shaking slightly like a monorail. When it was gone, Peter was left with nothing. He looked down at the rope again. Weighed it in his hands. It reminded him of the swings in the back garden at home, that had been there since his sons were young, and were still there, used now by their kids, his grandkids. How the hell did all that happen? When, where, how did he become a granddad? It didn't feel as if it was possible.

Rope like this one he held in his hands now hung the swings from the bright-red frame back in Peter's garden. Except, lately, it had begun to feel less and less like it was Peter's garden. He had begun to feel less and less as if he belonged there, as if, even when he was physically there, sitting on the metal chairs by the metal table on the decking, he wasn't really there at all.

He knew something was happening to him. The only words he had for it were that he had fallen in love. So completely and utterly in love, that now it – she – had been taken away from him; had left him like a boat leaves land; he was barely there himself anymore. But Peter knew, just like he knew religion was a lie and kindness doesn't exist, that love was something he'd concocted inside himself. It had nothing to do with that girl. It was just an old man's need. An uncomfortable truth that he faced and felt fall inside him like a long held breath. Maybe a part of him had died already. Maybe what he was thinking wasn't so bad. Because maybe the bit that mattered most in a person was already gone in him, and the bit he would be finishing off wasn't all that important anyway.

*

The woman told Kate to wait outside the office while she made the call.

"What did you say is wrong with him?" she asked her.

Kate could hear words fighting inside her as she struggled with what to say. "I don't know," she said. "He said he wasn't feeling good, not well, but I... He really did seem quite ill. And I'm worried."

The woman looked at her doubtfully. “Well, OK,” she said. “I’ll call his wife, but you’ll have to wait outside.”

Outside the office, Kate stood with her back leaning against the wall. She tried to concentrate and listen in on the phone conversation, but all she could hear was a low muffled sound coming from the room.

After a few minutes the door opened again and the woman stood there. Kate lurched to a standing straight position and looked at the woman for information.

“I’ve told his wife and she’s going straight home now, so no need for you to worry, it’s all taken care of.”

*

You couldn’t use a climbing rope because of the give, the stretch. It wouldn’t work. Natural fibres were probably best. Hard-wearing, taut. It hurt more when placed against the skin and tied tightly. It scratched and caused bruising and burns, but none of that mattered to Peter at this stage.

He had selected the perfect length of rope from the stocks back at the factory. He’d waited till no one was around. Till the bloke in the trolley-like forklift had passed by, and the aisle Peter stood in was quiet. Then he’d found his rope, cut it, and he’d wound it round his hand till it formed an oversized, looped knuckle duster, and he’d taken it home.

*

Susie pressed “End Call” on her mobile. She’d just had the strangest conversation with someone at Peter’s work. Saying he was ill and she should go home now. Why would she do that?

She frowned as she still stared at the mobile phone, like the call was still inside it, like it would tell her what the hell that was all about.

He’d been all right this morning. He wasn’t ill this morning.

She looked down at the supermarket trolley in front of her, half-full with boxes of cereal and loaves of bread and those cakes Anthony liked. She'd finish up here and then head home. She was going to do that anyway, so it was no bother.

*

She'd wanted to run. She'd watched the door and the phone and the clock all day. She'd wanted to get up and run, do something, find him, make sure he was OK. But she couldn't find him. So there was nowhere she could run.

She'd carried on with her work for as long as she could. Half expected a tap on the shoulder. Half expected the police. Hoped it could be him walking in and smiling and telling her he'd been stupid. Didn't mean it.

Kate had worked for as long as she could, but it was no use.

She said she felt ill and she went home early. A couple of people made a remark about how there must be something going round, a virus mingling with the sound of the photocopier and the smell of women's perfume and coffee from the little kitchen. Must be, they said, she wasn't the only one to go home sick that day.

Kate had nodded. She could feel the strained look on her own face and she could see their reaction when people looked at her. They thought she must be feeling really ill. She went home. And she waited.

Later that day she would receive a phone call about Peter's death and the next day be visited at home by a senior manager from the rope factory. And she would be told that Peter had used rope taken from the factory. And she would be asked if she'd known. And she'd cry. And she'd say no, she'd swear it, no she didn't know. He'd told her he didn't feel well, said he felt really ill, and that was all.

*

It didn't feel like Christmas. It wasn't cold enough. The sky was too bright and fairy lights too sparse.

Melanie had toyed with the idea of going home, seeing friends and family, feeling the familiar chill of the season, hearing Christmas songs playing on a loop in shops. Maybe it would even snow. But in the end she'd decided to stay where she was. Couldn't face going back again.

The drive to the factory was an odd one today. It had been on her mind since she woke up. She was aware of the dreams that circled her head all night and the slightly uneasy feeling she'd had all morning. But still, she couldn't quite pin it down. It was nothing really. She didn't even know why the nagging pulse of something being wrong was with her. There was nothing wrong.

Melanie's life and career had been on an upward journey ever since she'd moved to Portugal. She'd moved on in the rope company. Even more than she'd expected. Even quicker than her old boss back in Lyme had predicted. She seemed to fit right in here, and she'd found a nice apartment to rent and bought a car. Life was good here. The Portuguese weather felt like a constant smile, even in winter it was never too cold, never bitter like it was back in England. And she was still living by the sea, the twinkle of it never too far from her.

So, why did she feel out of sorts this morning? Why was there a nudge of anxiousness in her blood today?

*

He looked all around him for a way forward when it was all over. A way to move on. Get past it. Make a start at least. In the end there had only been one way he could see. When something as bad as that happened, you either got as far away as possible and made a completely new start, put it behind you, or you got right in there with it all, in the heart of it, and you worked your way through. Anthony had decided to do the latter.

It wasn't because he didn't miss his dad. In fact he missed him in ways he didn't think were possible. But a year had passed and Peter was still with him every day. That was

Anthony's choice, his way of dealing with it. He was still with all of them, of course, but not so literally as he was with Anthony.

Anthony's brothers had their own lives, separate; they had their own families but they missed their dad just as much. They'd all come round to the house on what would have been Peter's birthday and they'd talked about him for hours, pouring out memories from when they were kids, laughing at shared jokes about things he'd said and nodding each time one of them remembered something else.

And his mum, she kept Peter's picture on the sideboard in the hallway and, Anthony had noticed, one by her bed. It was like she never let him out of sight for too long, like she had to keep him there in one way or another.

They all did. It was a balancing act. Not letting him go while finding their own ways to get on with their lives. It was like people always say, you don't know how much you'll miss someone until they're gone.

He drove to Bridport every day and he thought about the route. The wheels of his car following those of his dad's, his footprints when he walked in the factory crossing his. He thought he had, at last, made his dad proud. This was what Peter wanted all along. This was what he'd hoped Anthony would do. Follow the family line. Work with rope. Make him proud. After all that had happened, Anthony thought it was the least he could do. But in a strange way, he was doing it for himself now, not for his dad. It had given him a purpose. And more than anything now, that's what Anthony needed. A new beginning.

*

Kate stood for a second with her thinly gloved hands held up in the air in front of her as if they were covered in poison instead of tuna from the sandwich she was making.

"You know I can't let you have it," she said. "You've got to pay like everyone else or I'll get in trouble."

Matthew grinned at her. "I know, I'm going to pay, don't worry."

Kate looked back down at the sandwich, half prepared, and began placing lettuce and tomato on top of the tuna.

She'd worked in the tearooms down in Lyme for eight months now. It was different. Very different to what she was used to doing at the rope factory. There were always people in the tearooms, in and out, chatting, to each other and to Kate. She liked that. She never seemed to be bored here. Never found herself gazing out of the window and feeling the lack of fresh air, or watching the clock for break and home time. It was always busy, and even when there was a lull in customers there was so much to do, clearing tables, loading the dishwasher, preparing food. It gave Kate little time to think about anything else, and in the end that was what she'd needed. She'd tried to carry on at the rope factory, but time didn't make it any easier. She needed something different. Something she'd never done before. Something with less reminders.

"I could get used to this," Matthew joked.

Kate laughed, her gaze still on the sandwich. They'd made a deal. They'd got everything out in the open and they'd decided. They'd make a go of it. A new start. They'd spent months with the after-taste of arguments stale inside them, difficulties with words and circling each other's moods. It was make or break. In the end that's what she'd said. It was give up on it or start again. They started again. No more secrets, they'd both said. No lies. Nothing hidden. And since Kate had left the factory and started her new job here she felt everything had lifted.

*

She drove the road up to the factory with the radio on. Portuguese words and phrases were beginning to sound normal and familiar to her now. She'd picked up the basics really quickly and the details of those sounds and pronunciations were starting to follow.

She turned the car off the main road and up to the factory, found her parking space and turned off the engine. The radio breathed its last for now, the station presenter just fitting in his intro to the next song: "Peter..."

It happened just as she turned off the radio, the car quiet in the cool morning. She shook herself and opened the door. The factory was tall in the grey sky and the slow soft fall of rain could be heard all around her.

That's what it was. She realised it as soon as she stood up, moments after hearing his name in a foreign mouth in another country. The last word from the radio before it died. It was a year ago. It was this time last year.

It had taken his name being spoken on the radio for her to be reminded it had all happened only a year ago. That was how much she'd moved on.

She closed the car door behind her and began walking across the yard to the entrance of the factory. She'd moved as far away as she could from her old life. She'd left them all behind, Susie, Anthony, Peter. This was what was best for her. This was best for Melanie. It sounded selfish as she thought it, but then, she'd realised, everyone is selfish. Everyone does the things that work for them at the time. Just like Peter. It had taken Melanie a little while to come around to this way of thinking, but she was surviving, sink or swim. She was swimming. That was her decision. Move away, have a good life, move on. Peter had decided to sink. And that wasn't Melanie's fault. It was Peter's life, she thought, and he'd done what he wanted to do with it. It was no one else's fault.

*

Kate had been right, that first time he'd met her, when she said people aren't as different as they think they are. Anthony had spent his whole life thinking he was different, not good enough, not like everyone else, too weak, a failure, a disappointment to his dad. And he'd thought, stupidly, that had been why Peter had done what he did. But people really aren't that different. Anthony saw that now. People are people, they make their own decisions, and no one was to blame for someone else's actions. He felt able to get on with his life, with his dad always still with him. And he didn't feel responsible anymore.

*

She'd almost done with the sandwich she was making for Matt. She'd cut through the bread and lettuce, her hand pressing down on the knife, and she was just about to put it onto a plate when she got a jolt.

Her boss was moving from the kitchen behind her out to where the tables and chairs were. He was talking to the other woman who worked there. "Can you believe it's a year?" he said.

"Is it?"

"Yeah, of course, it was Christmas, wasn't? If you remember, it was the funeral just when I was sorting out who got what time off at Christmas. Remember?"

"Oh yeah."

"Terrible time for it. I mean, there's no good time, is there, but Christmas. Terrible time for... to lose someone... and the way..."

Kate slid the sandwich onto the plate without looking up. There would be reminders. There was no avoiding that. People would mention it, but with each month that passed she had found a growing sense of peace about the whole thing. As long as she and Matthew remained solid she felt she could cope with anything.

She'd felt to blame at the time, but now, with some distance between herself and those events, she could see that there was nothing she could have done. Peter had made up his mind. He'd made his own choices. And that wasn't Kate's fault. That wasn't anyone's fault.

The little bell above the door rang as a customer walked in. There was a waft of cold air and the fairy lights around the door strained and shook. Kate looked up. Standing there was a uniformed policeman, his radio crackling with a far-off voice. He put his hand to the radio to turn down the volume slightly then he moved forward towards the counter. As he stood there Kate lifted the plate with the sandwich on ready to hand it to Matthew. She looked at where Matthew had been standing a moment ago, but he'd turned the other way and was looking out of the window. Kate was sure she could feel something. Something not quite right. Something in the way he was standing, his face turned away, his body tense.

"Matthew," she said. He turned back and she handed him the sandwich. There was a slight tinge to his skin, a fizzing of nerves, things he held within himself fighting under the surface. For a minute she was sure she could see it. Then she looked at the policeman. He held his arms tight by his sides, his uniform bulky. He looked up at the board behind the counter.

"Are you eating in or taking away?" Kate asked.

"I'll take it away," he replied. "Busy day today."

*

He tied a good knot. A slipknot. He knew as much as the next bloke knew about slipknots. A noose. Knew the same as the next old bloke tired of bothering anymore. He threaded the rope, made a loop that looked a good size and was about to do it, about to slip it over his head. He wanted to die. He was so sure he wanted to die, and yet, at that one moment when he was staring it down, he suddenly found he couldn't do it. He looked at the rope in his hands. He wanted to die, but his body was telling him he didn't. A rush of something he couldn't ignore went through his blood and into his brain. I don't want to die. I don't want to die.

He grasped the rope tighter in his hands as a noise outside made his muscles jolt. There was someone outside the house.

*

Matthew would recognise that jeep anywhere. It was personal. It was connected to him now like the sight of an unpleasant neighbour or the bad memory of a scary film he'd seen as a teenager, or someone he'd gone to school with. It had a personal connection to Matthew and he'd know it instantly whenever he saw it.

This morning he'd seen it for the first time since it had been standing in the layby and Kate had got out of it.

He'd been in the van with his work-mate after finishing up on an old lady's house first thing in the morning. They were driving out of town to the next job when Matthew noticed it, near the top of Silver Street.

The jeep was passing along the top road, towards the border with Devon, and Matthew and his work-mate were now travelling directly behind it. It was unmistakable. There wasn't another quite like that around here, and Matthew would never forget it. He felt a sudden surge of anger at the sight of that vehicle, roaming around Lyme as if nothing had happened. The driver, whoever he was, clearly sauntering around without a care in the world. Maybe he gave lifts home to lots of women. Maybe he was at it all the time. Maybe he tried it on with everybody. Or maybe it was just Kate, maybe he'd targeted her specially. The thought of that made the knowing grip of jealousy squeeze hard at Matthew's insides. The bastard. Thought he could come along and take Matthew's girl away. Not a chance.

He watched as the jeep turned up a driveway towards a large house at the end of it. Matthew had the unstoppable feeling that he couldn't let Peter get away with all this.

"Pull over, will you?"

His work-mate glanced at him, then back at the road. "What? Why?"

"Just pull over, I need to... do something."

"What are you going on about? Do something? Do what?"

"There's something... I forgot, to pick up for Kate, something I said I'd get for Kate."

His work-mate turned into a driveway to the right and started moving the van around.

"What, you want me to go back down to the shops?"

Matthew hesitated "Yes, er… I suppose so, drop me down there... I'll ring you when I'm done."

"What? Are you serious? We've got to get to the job,

Matt, can't it wait till later?"

The impatience was growing in Matthew's voice. "No, it can't wait! Just drop me off, will you?"

His work-mate threw his hands up and then back down heavy on the steering wheel. "OK, whatever you say, just don't go blaming me if we're behind schedule today because you had to 'go to the shops'."

His work-mate turned the van around and drove back down Silver Street.

Matthew got out of the van and slammed the door shut. "I'll give you a call in a bit."

"Yeah, well, I can't just jump when you call, alright?" his work-mate shouted out of the window.

Matthew watched as the van drove up to the top of the road again and turned right. Then he walked furiously back up, as fast as he could, crossing the main road at the top and heading towards the house he'd seen the jeep go into.

He walked up the long pathway and onto the gravel drive without really knowing what he would do once he got there. He was too angry to think. His mind was too clouded with this unstoppable rage that seemed to live permanently in him lately. He stood there and looked up at the house. This was where the man lived.

Peter had let the rope fall from his grasp. It was definitely someone outside. Peter could hear feet shuffling in the gravel on the drive and he could see the shape of a man moving like liquid in the glass of the front door. It wasn't Susie or Anthony or anyone else he knew. They would either have let themselves in or knocked. This person was just hanging round outside.

He stood frozen for a minute. Then he looked down at the rope on the floor where he'd left it. He eyed it as if it couldn't be trusted. As if he needed to have it still in his view, know where it was and what it was up to. Then he walked slowly forward and opened the front door.

Matthew had his hands in his pockets and looked up from where his feet kicked the gravel as the front door to the house opened. It took him a minute to place the man. At first he thought it was just the jeep thing, just the layby incident, and his mind was making a connection that wasn't there. But then he remembered. He knew this guy. Well, he didn't know him, but he'd met him before. Years ago, when he was still at school. Oh yeah, he'd met him before alright, he remembered this guy and all the trouble he'd got Matthew into.

Peter stood there and stared at him in a strange vacant way.

"What do you want?" he asked.

The man looked tired, done in. It only made Matthew feel stronger.

"I want to talk to you," he said. He walked forward, intending on barging into the house, but Peter moved easily aside and let him pass.

Once inside the house Matthew looked around. Peter had followed him back in and had closed the door. The rope lay in its slipknot on the carpet and Matthew looked down at it.

"What's this?" he asked.

Peter sighed. "What's it look like?"

Matthew made an over-exaggerated look of surprise. "You thinking of doing yourself in?"

"I was."

Matthew shoved his hands back in his pockets and rocked on his heels. "Well, don't let me stop you. No, I think it's a good idea. After the way you've done your best to mess up my life, can't say you'd be missed."

Peter was staring at this man. His whole body felt pulled to the ground by weights and nothing mattered. He'd let a stranger walk into his house and stood talking to him now about God knows what, and it didn't matter at all. Maybe it was the rope. Maybe he should just try another way. Maybe he did really want to die and it had just been the fear of the rope that stopped him.

"What are you talking about?" he said.

"You," Matthew answered. Then a smile spread on his face and he let go a small laugh. "You don't remember me, do you?"

Peter was frowning now.

"That holiday. Years ago. I was a mate of Anthony's, well, I say mate... anyway, me and Stu came on that holiday and there was that trouble..."

Matthew almost smiled at the look on Peter's face. It was almost worth it just to see him squirm. This man, Peter, who had been the cause of so much bother for Matthew. Right back to when he was a teenager and he'd been on holiday that time with Peter's son, Anthony. Matthew had been Stuart's friend really. Stuart was alright. A bit of a dick sometimes, but alright. Anthony's parents had said he could take two friends on their holiday and of course he'd pick Stuart, he wouldn't dare not to and, anyway, it wasn't like Anthony had any other friends. And of course if Stuart was going so was Matthew. That holiday had been a complete disaster. After what happened at that bar with him and Stuart going on a bit of a rampage down there, Matthew had got into loads of trouble back at home. Peter just couldn't leave it be, could he? He had to tell their parents. Stuart's parents didn't give a toss, but Matthew's... they'd barely let him take a step sideways for ages after that.

The memory faded slowly into Peter's head, showing itself on his face.

"...And you drove me and Stu home and told our parents, remember?"

"Yes, I remember," Peter said. "But, why...?"

"Why am I here now? Kate. That's why."

"Kate?"

"Yeah, you messing with my life a bit when I was a kid is one thing, but you messing with *this* now, I can't forgive that."

"You and Kate?"

"Yes, me and Kate! She's the best thing that's ever happened to me, she's *my* girlfriend and I'm not gonna stand by and watch you having a crack at her!"

"I didn't... I mean, we didn't... I'm fond of her."

"Fond of her? Come on. You didn't seriously think anything would happen, did you? An old fart like you. Why would she ever be interested in a sad ugly old git like you? In fact, why would anyone be interested in you?"

He looked down at the rope and was instantly aware of Peter's eyes following his. "I mean it," he said. "Who would miss you? The kind of guy who rats on teenage kids to their parents. The kind of guy who sneaks around letching on girls half their age. Your poor wife must be appalled. She must regret the day she met you. And your sons, what must they think? Having a dad like you!"

They were looking from the rope to each other as Matthew spoke, Peter's eyes flitting to the rope in its cosy curl on the floor more and more, the words Matthew had uttered worming in his brain, making his heart feel older and more and more useless, pointless. Matthew watching him, till he said, "We'd all be better off without you. Do it! Go on, pick it up, do it!"

Peter could see Matthew's hatred. He really wanted him to do it.

"You're a useless waste of space. You know it!"

He did know it. It's what he'd been feeling. He knew it was true.

"Just do everyone a favour and end it!"

Peter lurched forward and picked up the rope. It was happening fast now. He knew better this time than to stop and think about it. The old dragging feeling of nothing hollowing him out. He was quick with the slipknot, his hands going through the same familiar actions they had less than a quarter of an hour before, but this time he wouldn't stop. Matthew's relentless words dug into him and made the end seem more urgent.

"Nobody cares!"

He was aware of him still standing there, watching, spurring him on. Do it.

"Nobody loves you, nobody will miss you!"

Peter didn't give himself a chance to find a way back now. He secured the rope quickly and let his body fall.

Matthew felt seconds stretch and the air move around him too fast. He was aware of his mouth quivering and his hands shaking, though he couldn't instantly make sense of it. He was rooted for he didn't know how many minutes, before he could take his eyes away from the hanging, slumped body of Peter, to other areas of the room. He looked at the door first. He had to get out of here. His brain began to turn over the practicalities of the situation he was in. Survival was all that mattered. He pulled the sleeve of his jacket over his hand and moved slowly to the door. There he turned the handle, covered by material, quietly made his way out, and left Peter inside.

*

He would have seen the car turn in the drive, maybe even seen it slowly coming closer up from the road, if he'd still been there. He would have heard the tyres crunch on the gravel and the handbrake being put in place.

Susie got out of the car and slammed the door. She walked around to the boot and took her shopping bags out, the thin plastic handles stretching against her palms. Carrying the bags in one hand, she put her car keys into her pocket and walked to the front door. She pushed her shoulder against the door. It didn't open. She stood back and looked up. Maybe he wasn't home after all. Maybe he'd felt OK and gone back to work. She took her keys back out of her pocket and unlocked the door.

It only took a second. The carrier bags dropped heavily beside her, a tub of cream and a circle of Sellotape rolling out and onto the hallway floor.

She could hear herself scream.

Also available from Armley Press

Coming Out as a Bowie Fan in Leeds, Yorkshire, England
By Mick McCann
ISBN 0-9554699-0-2

Hot Knife
By John Lake
ISBN 0-9554699-1-0

Nailed – Digital Stalking in Leeds, Yorkshire, England
By Mick McCann
ISBN 0-955469-2-9

How Leeds Changed the World – Encyclopaedia Leeds
By Mick McCann
ISBN 0-955469-3-0

Blowback
By John Lake
ISBN 0-9554699-4-7

Speedbomb
By John Lake
ISBN 0-9554699-5-4

In All Beginnings
By Ray Brown
ISBN 0-9554699-6-1

Leeds, The Biography: A History of Leeds in Short Stories
By Chris Nickson
ISBN 0-9554699-7-X

Lightning Source UK Ltd.
Milton Keynes UK
UKOW02f1850080615

253117UK00002B/36/P